FAMILY GRANDSTAND

ALSO BY CAROL RYRIE BRINK

FAMILY SABBATICAL

Family Grandstand

BY CAROL RYRIE BRINK

ILLUSTRATED BY JEAN MACDONALD PORTER

THE VIKING PRESS

NEW YORK

THIS BOOK IS FOR

SUSAN CAROL HUNTER

AND

CAROL PHILLIPS

AND ALL THE CAROLS AND SUSANS

WHO ENJOY THEIR NAMES

Contents

I.	They Had a Hero and a Tower	11
II.	The Strange Behavior of Tommy Tucker	21
III.	'Twas Friday Night	30
IV.	Busy Saturday	39
V.	How to Cross a Street	48
VI.	Tower Seats	59
VII.	The Thousand and One Nights	70
VIII.	Happy Birthday, Dear Georgie!	80
IX.	An Ad in the Paper	90
X.	Tutor for Tommy	101
XI.	Leaping Lizard	113
XII.	A Turtle Picnic	125
XIII.	A Ghostly Idea	135
XIV.	Free as the Air	143
XV.	Mice and Flowers	152
XVI.	Whose Dog?	168
XVII.	More about the Lizard	178
XVIII.	North River Street	185
XIX.	Concerning Dean Ambrose	190
XX.	A Number of Things	198

FAMILY GRANDSTAND

I. They Had a Hero and a Tower

A wonderful thing had happened to the Ridgeway children during the summer, and now that it was fall some of the glory and importance of the summer still clung to them. The wonderful thing that had happened to them was that they had had a football hero to mow their lawn.

Mother had a funny way of saying things, and she used to say, when anyone asked her where they lived, "We live on College Avenue and we have the football stadium in our laps." Of course, then either Susan or George had to explain, "The stadium isn't *really* in our laps. It's a block and a half down the street."

But with the stadium so near, the Ridgeway children could not help being interested in football. And now that Tommy Tucker was considered the greatest quarterback that the Midwest team had ever had, the Ridgeway children could say proudly, "He mowed our lawn last summer."

Even in the summer Tommy Tucker had been the children's hero. Boys and girls from all up and down the street had come to see him mowing the Ridgeway lawn.

"We could charge admission," George had said, "and make a lot of money."

But Susan had said, "No. This is a free treat we can give the other children. It would be wrong to charge."

Professor Ridgeway's front yard had a low stone wall all around it, and the children could sit on this wall and watch Tommy mow, just as the grownups sat around the big stadium down the street on a Saturday afternoon in the fall watching him play football.

"I could print tickets with my rubber stamp set," George had continued. George was going on ten and had quite a talent for business. "It would be real easy to collect the tickets at the front gate."

But twelve-year-old Susan had been firm. "No," she had said, "this is our treat."

Dumpling, who was six, had said nothing. Dumpling was

really named Irene, but because of her roundness in the middle she had never been called anything but Dumpling. She was very quiet, but the glasses that she wore gave her a reputation for wisdom and learning. She did not have to speak; she only had to look thoughtful to impress people.

Like Dumpling, who was never called Irene, Tommy Tucker had another name which was very seldom used. His real name was Thomas Tokarynski, but few people could either pronounce or spell it. It was very difficult when he made a splendid run with the football and scored a touchdown for Midwest University to shout:

> "Thomas Tokarynski!
> Thomas Tokarynski!
> Rah! Rah! Rah!"

It was more like sneezing or coughing than cheering and could not easily be done. But one day someone had shouted, "Yay, Tom Tokar!" and someone else had shouted, "Yay, Tommy Tucker!"

The whole crowd of football fans had taken it up, and ever since he had been called by that name. There were all sorts of good yells that went with Tommy Tucker.

> "Rah! Rah! Rah! Tucker! Tucker! Tucker!"
> "Tommy Tuck! Tommy Tuck! Tommy Tu—u—cker!"
> "Tuck into 'em, Tommy!"

and so forth.

Tommy Tucker was the shortest and lightest man on the football team, but his muscles were as hard as iron, and he was a wonderful runner. One had only to see how the lawn mower whizzed and the grass flew to understand that.

"Tommy," George would say, "let the kids feel your muscle, will you?" And sometimes, if he had time, Tommy would flex up his arm and let all the children feel it. The muscle was so hard that no one could make a dent in it.

George thought that he might at least have been allowed to print tickets for the privilege of feeling Tommy's muscle, but Susan always said no.

Susan was older than George and she was quite firm, but it was not so much her age or her firmness that made George and Dumpling accept her decisions. It was her good sense. Experience had taught them that Susan usually knew best. So George did not print up any tickets, and all summer long the sight of Tommy Tucker mowing the lawn was free to every child who cared to walk five to ten blocks to sit on the Ridgeway wall and watch.

Now that fall had come, and school and college had begun, the Ridgeway children did not see so much of Tommy Tucker. Sometimes they would hear his cheerful whistle in the distance, and they would see him going by to classes or football practice. Then he would greet them good-naturedly, tousle Dumpling's hair or make sparring motions at George, and pass on. For now he had no time to mow lawns.

However, this was one point on which they could not reason with Mother. She always called it her Ivory Tower, and if she did not say "far from the madding crowd," she said "far from the thundering herd."

"She means us by the thundering herd," said Susan, "but I don't know why the Tower should be ivory."

"I think," said Dumpling, "it must have something to do with soap." Whenever Dumpling made a remark the others stopped to think it over.

"Ivory soap?" asked Susan.

"Ninety-nine and forty-four hundredths per cent pure," said George.

"But why?" asked Susan.

"I don't know," Dumpling said.

All during the week the Tower belonged to Mother, but on Saturday afternoons she turned it over to the children.

The best part about the Tower was the view. You could look down into the back yard of Professor Jones of the Chemistry Department and see him tying up his prize chrysanthemums in the fall or digging for cutworms in the spring. You could see Dean Ambrose driving by in his shiny Studebaker.

Down the street you could see the Terrible Torrences, who were five and six years old, mixing up mud and water in one of their mother's mixing bowls to paint a large cartoon on the side of their white stucco house.

On the other side you could see the Gimmick kids, whose

In fact the Ridgeways' lawn was very seldom mowed, for Professor Ridgeway was busy too, and the grass grew long and green. The yellow leaves fell on it from the big elm trees along College Avenue. The little maple tree at the side of the house turned a perfect scarlet, and the elm behind the carriage house turned gold. It was the loveliest time of year in Midwest City.

Now instead of Tommy the Ridgeway children had Dorothy Sturm, and they did not like Dorothy so well. Dorothy was eighteen and she was a very good student, but she did not have enough money to go to college unless she worked for her room and board. So that fall she had come with her cardboard suitcase and her box of books to live at the Ridgeways' house and to help Mother with the housework while Mother finished writing her mystery novel.

Dorothy might easily have replaced Tommy in the children's affections, but somehow she didn't. The trouble with Dorothy was that she was always in a hurry getting things done. When the children came around to ask her questions or to tell her what they had been doing, Dorothy just said, "Scram!" or sometimes, "Am-scray!" She did not say it unkindly, but as if she had too many more important things on her mind to be bothered.

Dorothy knew how to peel potatoes with the fewest possible motions of the hands and the least waste of potato. She made a bed quite well in one minute by going only twice on each side of it, while Mother drifted like a cloud around and around it, thinking her own thoughts, and taking a long time.

"Dorothy is a jewel," Mother said. But the children thought Dorothy might have been more fun.

The Ridgeways had a nice big yard, and their house was the oldest one in the block. Mother said it had been built in the year one, but that was just her funny way of saying 1895. It was a wonderful house. It had both front and back stairways, so the children could chase each other up the front stairway, through the upper hall and down the back stairway, through the kitchen, the pantry, the front hall, and up the front stairs again. There was never any place where they had to stop and turn around and retrace their steps.

There were all sorts of places for hiding in the old house, if one wanted to play hiding games, and on the first landing of the front stairway was a remarkable window. It was all made of oddly shaped pieces of colored glass. There was a window seat below it, and Susan and George and Dumpling could kneel on the window seat and look out through the different-colored pieces of glass.

"My world is red," cried George. "I see a red man and a red dog."

"I'm green," said Susan. "The man and the dog are green."

And Dumpling would say, "Blue, like the sky, mine is a fairy tale."

"Why a fairy tale?" asked the others.

"I don't know," said Dumpling.

The basement of the house was dark and mys a number of rooms and a great fat furnace, wh to cling to the ceiling with many legs like a spi spring the water came into the basement in a boxes bobbed merrily around on the tide. Then th put on their boots and sailed boats. But in the f dry and pleasant, and Father had a work benc room, and George had another room for winte guinea pigs, his rabbits, and his white rats.

But the most interesting thing about the Rid house was that it had a Tower. No one that they had a house with a Tower. There were stairs an that got narrower and narrower. They went past th where the old *National Geographics* were piled, and you could hear the music of the rain on a dark a day. On up, on up, went the stairs into the little T There were five windows all around the Tower with a of bird's-eye view of the whole neighborhood. Mother a desk up there with a pile of yellow paper, her typewr a wastebasket, a pencil sharpener, and a lot of pencils.

"This is my Ivory Tower," Mother said, "far from madding crowd."

"But the Tower is made of wood, Mother," George sai and Susan said, "Mother, I always thought the word wa 'maddening.'"

house was almost as old as the Ridgeways' but did not have
a Tower, taking apart an old bicycle in their back yard.

But from the east window there was the most wonderful
view of all. A block away, down the street, you could see
right over the wall of the football stadium and onto the
playing field. With Father's old field glasses you could follow every play and even read the numbers on the backs of
the players. Tommy Tucker's number was 25.

At this season of the year everybody in Midwest City
was more or less interested in football. Everybody wanted
Midwest University to win its games against Coronia and
Michigan and Iowa and Wisconsin and the other schools
represented in the football conference.

Thousands of cars jammed College Avenue on a Saturday
afternoon when there was a game in the stadium; thousands
of people with pennants flying and chrysanthemums pinned
on their coats hurried by to get seats in the stadium. The
roar of the cheering could be heard for many blocks in all
directions. Popcorn wagons whistled invitingly on every
corner, and the Gimmick boys did a very profitable business
parking cars in their driveway and back yard at 25 cents
a car.

George, and even Susan, wanted very much to park cars
in the Ridgeways' back yard or to sell something to the
crowds, but Father would never let them.

"We could certainly use a little money, Daddy," George
said wistfully.

"That's true," said Professor Ridgeway, "but we have a certain academic dignity to maintain."

"If we can't park cars we could sell popcorn," George suggested.

"No! No!" said Father. "What would Dean Ambrose say if he knew that the children of one of his professors were hawking and vending on the street?"

"What is hawking and vending?" asked Dumpling with interest.

"Selling things," said Susan.

"And what is adachemic dignity?" Dumpling wanted to know.

"Academic dignity," said Mother, "is an imaginary line, like the equator, that separates our house from the Gimmicks' house."

"No, no," said Father. "We're no better than the Gimmicks, not a bit. But Mr. Gimmick has his own auto repair shop; he doesn't need to think how it looks to other people if his boys sell things on the streets. On the other hand, we represent a great University; we have to think how all of our public actions will look to other people."

But even if they couldn't sell things, the Ridgeway children had their own private Tower for watching the games, and all summer long a football hero had mowed their lawn!

II

The Strange Behavior of Tommy Tucker

On a Friday afternoon at the beginning of October the Ridgeway children were walking slowly home from school in the pleasant sunshine.

"Game tomorrow," George said. "Oh, boy! And then on Sunday—on *Sunday*, you know what?"

"Your birthday," said Susan, feeling just a little bored. "You've only told me fifteen times, George."

"Well, I'm glad you remember," he answered hopefully.

"We ought to hurry," Susan said. "We have to rake the leaves this afternoon."

"I can't hurry, my legs ache."

"We could hurry if there was ice cream," Dumpling said. They stopped and looked at her, for what she said was quite true.

The Gimmick boys caught up with the Ridgeways. They did not have to rake, so they were in a hurry to get home.

"Hello," they said.

"Hello," said the Ridgeways. The Gimmick boys, Tim and Tad, were the same ages as Susan and George.

"We're going to make some swell new signs for parking cars," Tim said.

"We're going to make like a big cut-out hand pointing a thumb at our back yard. You know, like you thumb a ride, kind of," said Tad.

"And print, 'Parking twenty-five cents,'" said Tim.

"Swell," said Susan wistfully, and George said, "Gee!"

The Gimmicks hurried by.

Soon the Terrible Torrences came up behind.

"Susan is our sit-ter! Susan is our sit-ter!" they chanted.

"Ssh! Ssh! Ssh!" said Susan. She did not like to be reminded in public that she was the Torrences' sitter. It was not that she was ashamed of being a baby sitter, for that was an honorable profession, and she adored babies. She was ashamed *for* the Torrences who, at five and six, should have been old enough to look after themselves without a sitter. But Mrs. Torrence was always afraid that they would burn down the house or kill the cat or ruin the plumbing if she left them in the house alone. So Susan had to look after them when Professor and Mrs. Torrence went out to dinner or the movies.

"We are going to dig a hole in our back yard," said Alvin, the larger of the two Terrible Torrences.

"A great big hole," said Rudy, "big enough for all the houses in the neighborhood to fall into."

"Our house too?" asked Susan.

"Every house on College Avenue," said Alvin.

"Listen, Alvin and Rudy," said George in a sweet and gentle voice, "how would you like to rake leaves? At our house? You wouldn't have to pay us a thing."

"Would Tommy Tucker be there?"

The Ridgeways shook their heads regretfully.

"Then we'd rather dig a hole for all the houses to fall into," said the Terrible Torrences, rushing on.

"That settles it," Susan said. "We'd better hurry right along and get the raking done as fast as we can. That's the best way."

Raking was really a very pleasant thing to do on a beautiful fall day. The yellow leaves rustled and murmured underfoot. They smelled sweet and warm and dry. More yellow leaves floated gently down from time to time. They floated past the tower where Mother's typewriter was going *clickety-clack, clickety-clack!* They settled easily on the long green grass.

At first Susan and George raked the leaves into long rows, and then they discovered that by raking other rows crosswise they could make imaginary rooms with leaf walls. In one they made a bedroom with a big leaf bed, and Dumpling lay down on it with her old rag doll, Irene, and they covered her with leaves. They began to sing as they worked, one of Father's favorite songs:

> " 'Twas Friday night when we set sail,
>   And our ship not far from the land,
>   When there we espied a pretty mermaid
>   With a comb and a glass in her hand."

Soon the Gimmick boys finished their signs and came to sit on the wall and watch the Ridgeways rake. The Terrible Torrences found it more work than it was worth to dig a hole large enough to swallow the neighborhood, so they came too. They all began to sing:

> " 'Twas Friday night when we set sail,
>   And our ship not far from the land—"

They were all singing at the top of their lungs when Tommy Tucker came by. He began to sing too, and he stood and looked over the wall at the long grass and the ridges and piles of leaves.

The children were perfectly delighted. They stopped singing to cry, "Hi, Tommy! Hello, Tommy! Oh, Tommy, Tommy Tucker!"

"What are you doing?" asked Tommy.

"Raking the lawn."

"That's a funny way to do it," Tommy said.

"Well, we were playing a little as we raked," explained Susan. "I expect we will get it all cleaned up before suppertime."

"And *look* at that grass!" Tommy said gloomily. "I bet it hasn't been mowed since last summer."

"Not since you started to go to school and practice football, Tommy," said George.

Tommy shook his head sadly. "Get busy and clean off those leaves," he said, "and I'll mow."

The Ridgeway children began to rake like mad. The leaf walls crumbled and tumbled together. Dumpling and her doll were hastily raked out of their leaf bed and left high and dry. The Gimmick boys rushed home for extra rakes. Even the Terrible Torrences began clutching up armfuls of leaves and running with them to the burning-basket in the back alley. A lawn was never more quickly or enthusiastically cleaned of its leaves.

While they worked, Tommy went to the old carriage house that the Ridgeways used as a garage and wheeled out the lawn mower. It had developed a loud squeak, and he went back and found the oil can and gave it a good oiling. By the time he was ready to mow, the children had cleared one whole side of the lawn. Dorothy was looking out of the window at them, but she did not come out.

"Look, Tommy, what a good job we did! Look how we cleaned it, Tommy."

"Uh-huh," Tommy said. His mind seemed to be on other things today. He did not tousle Dumpling's hair or make sparring motions at George. He did not make jokes or shout, "Let's go, gang!" or "Out of my track, kids!" It was the first time that they had ever seen Tommy Tucker when he did not seem happy. Some of his gloom began to settle on the children. They did not sing as they worked, and they looked at him shyly to see what was the matter.

"Didn't you win the football game last week, Tommy?" asked Rudy Torrence. The Terrible Torrences always asked whatever came into their heads without stopping to think.

"Of course he won!" cried the Ridgeways and the Gimmicks. "What do you think?"

"You always win, don't you, Tommy?" said George proudly.

Usually if anyone asked him that Tommy Tucker said, "Sure, you bet!" But today he was quite serious. He said, "Oh, I wouldn't say that." He went on mowing the lawn, and the long green grass flew up like water in a fountain.

When the children had finished raking the leaves they sat on the wall and watched. The *clickety-clack* of Mother's typewriter in the Tower was drowned out completely by the *whirr-whizzity-bang* of the lawn mower. The children's eyes followed Tommy Tucker as he raced around the lawn. He was a wonderfully neat mower. He never left a little ridge of standing grass between mowed strips as some mowers do. Every blade of grass fell where it should. Susan could not help thinking of the barber who clipped George's hair in the summer, when Mother let him wear it quite short.

Tommy was approaching the wall where they sat, and

to break the gloom which had settled over them with Tommy's unusual silence Susan called out, "Tommy, you'd make a good barber."

Tommy stopped so suddenly that the children almost fell off the wall. He mopped his forehead with his handkerchief.

"You're right, sister," he said to Susan in an angry-sounding voice, "I'd make a good barber. I'm a good lawn mower. That's just about my speed."

"Well," said Susan, "you're the world's best football player too. We watch you from our Tower. I don't know what our team would do without you."

"I don't either," said Tommy frankly, "but they'd better begin to find out. They'd better begin to find out, that's all I have to say."

"Oh!" cried all of the children in terrible surprise. Tommy began to mow again, and they couldn't get another word out of him.

When he had finished the lawn, he wheeled the mower back to the garage.

"I'll go and call Mother and have her pay you," said Susan.

"No," Tommy said, "I don't want to be paid this time. I was just letting off steam."

"Letting off steam?" asked the Torrences. "We thought you were mowing the lawn."

"But Mother would want you to be paid," insisted Susan.

For the first time that afternoon Tommy Tucker smiled.

"Well, I'll tell you," he said, "if there are any of those good doughnuts your mother makes—"

Dorothy was in the kitchen peeling potatoes for supper when they all went in. She kept right on peeling potatoes as if a football hero were just the same as anybody else.

"Dorothy, look! This is Tommy Tucker," Susan said.

"Tucker?" said Dorothy as if she had never heard the name before.

"It's Tokarynski really," said George. "The football player. Don't you know?"

"Oh," said Dorothy.

"This is Dorothy Sturm, Tommy," said Susan.

"Oh," said Tommy. They did not seem to be very much interested in meeting each other.

"Let's take the doughnuts out on the back steps," Susan said tactfully. The doughnut jar was quite full when it came out. Tommy sat down on the back doorstep with George on one side of him and Dumpling on the other. The rest of the children sat around him in a circle on the freshly clipped lawn. The doughnut jar went around and around the circle. Presently it was nearly empty.

The Terrible Torrences, entirely full of doughnuts, were just beginning to put doughnuts in their pockets when Susan said, "Maybe we better leave one or two in the bottom of the jar for a nest egg, sort of."

Tommy got up and sighed. They could see that, although he had been sitting so near them, he had not been thinking about them at all. He looked at the nearly empty jar, and he said, "I hope your mother won't mind. But she sure is a wonderful doughnut maker."

"She's good at whatever she does," said George proudly.

"I wish I was," said Tommy Tucker. After that he went away down the walk without saying good-by. Outside the gate he began to whistle. It seemed that Tommy Tucker could never walk along without whistling. But today the tune he whistled was not gay. It sounded very much like a funeral march.

III

'Twas Friday Night

"Mother," Susan said before dinner, "I hope you won't mind about all the doughnuts being gone. But Tommy Tucker wouldn't take any other pay for mowing the lawn, and then the Gimmicks and the Terrible Torrences were here, and they had worked too."

"Doughnuts are intended to be eaten," Mother said, "and fortunately I had a few more than I could put in the jar. I have them on a plate in the top of the cupboard, so Father will get his share."

"M-m-m!" said Professor Ridgeway to the children. "Your mother is a wonderful woman."

They all sat down to dinner, and while they were eating Mrs. Ridgeway said, "Now it's Friday night—"

The children and Professor Ridgeway burst out singing:

" 'Twas Friday night when we set sail,
And our ship not far from the land—"

Dorothy looked at them in surprise because she was not used to living with people who sang at the table.

"Hush, hush!" said Mrs. Ridgeway. "This is serious. It's Friday night, and I think that we had better begin to plan our Saturday. There are quite a lot of things we have to do, and when the football crowd begins to surge by we might as well be living on a desert island in a raging sea. There is no getting in or out of our driveway—"

"So we might as well park cars, Mother," said George, but Susan said, "Ssh!"

"On Saturday morning Dumpling has to go to the Child Study Clinic and get her annual test," continued Mother, "and who will go with her?"

"I will, Mother," said Susan. "But why does it always have to be the Ridgeway children that they practice on? First it was me, and then it was George."

"Well, we're so handy here," said Mother, "it's nice and easy for them. I guess they keep a record of the family. They have a grocer's family and an insurance agent's family and a farmer's family, and so on. We're the professor's family."

"But why?" asked George.

"They are trying to learn all about children," said Professor Ridgeway. "It's a science, like zoology."

"I see," said George, "and we're the guinea pigs."

"Oh, George," cried Mother, "did you remember to feed your guinea pigs?"

"Yes, Mother," said George.

"And the white rats and the rabbits?"

"Oh, yes. They've got a real nice supper of fresh grass."

"And I fed the canary bird," said Dumpling. Everybody stopped and thought about this, although it was Dumpling's regular job for which she received ten cents a week.

"Well, bless your little heart!" cried Mother, and the others said, "Oh, good!" Dumpling continued to eat her dinner.

"Well, to get back to Saturday," said Mother. "So Susan will take Dumpling to the Child Study Clinic at the University, and George will clean the animal crates and go to the barber and get his hair cut, and Dorothy can use the vacuum cleaner while I do the marketing—"

"And how about Sunday?" asked George.

"Sunday?" asked Mother in surprise.

"Oh, my goodness, Mother," said George, "don't you remember what day Sunday is?"

"It can't be Christmas," said Mrs. Ridgeway with a twinkle in her eye. "It's too early in the season."

"For the same reason it can hardly be Thanksgiving," said Professor Ridgeway.

Susan began to giggle. "Maybe it's Halloween," she said.

"Oh, my goodness!" wailed George. "Doesn't anybody remember what day it is?"

"I know," said Dumpling. "It's George's birthday!"

"No!" cried the others, just as if they had not been reminded by George every day for weeks. "No! It can't be!"

"Yes, it is," said Dumpling.

"I didn't mean to remind you," said George politely, "only I just thought maybe some of you might be wanting to go downtown on Saturday to do some shopping or something, and it would be too bad if you forgot."

"That's true," said Mother. "How about it, Susan? Do you and Dumpling want to go downtown after you are through at the Child Study Clinic?"

"I think we'd better," said Susan.

George beamed happily. He had a white, curved mustache of milk on his upper lip. "Oh, boy!" he said.

"But we'll be back in time for the game," said Susan.

"Yes, indeed," said Father. "See that you get here before the crowds begin to arrive. You might be lost or trampled on."

"Father," said Susan, "Tommy Tucker was very queer today when he was mowing the lawn. He didn't look a bit cheerful. And he said something about how the team had better learn to get along without him. What do you think he meant?"

"The poor young man is probably working too hard," said Mother. "It's really too bad he has to earn his way through college by doing odd jobs and by being night watchman at the flour mill. Besides that he has football practice and Saturday games, and then his studies and his examinations."

"There you have it in a nutshell," said Professor Ridgeway. "You name all the things that Tom Tokarynski has to do to stay in college and on the football team, and the very last things you mention are his studies and his examinations."

"But he's a hero, Daddy!" cried Susan.

"Heroes have to pass their examinations," said Professor Ridgeway, "just the same as other students."

"That's so," said Dorothy suddenly. She had been eating her dinner with her usual efficiency, but now she joined the conversation. "That Mr. Tokarynski, or whatever his name is, is in my chemistry class, and I can tell you he's going to flunk."

"Why, Dorothy," cried Susan, "you never even spoke to him today, not even when I introduced you."

"There are a hundred and fifty students in that class. He wouldn't remember *me*," Dorothy said.

"Flunk—plunk," said Dumpling. "What is flunk, Dorothy?"

"It means he isn't smart enough to pass his examinations," Dorothy said. "It means he's dumb and he's going to fail. No wonder he didn't look cheerful. I expect they'll take him off the football team."

"You mean you have to be extra smart to play football?" asked George.

"You have to pass your examinations," Father said. "If a man fails in his college work, it is an indication that he does not have any extra time to spend on football games. Studies come first."

"But they couldn't put him off the team *now*, could they, Father?" begged Susan.

"His case is rather peculiar," said her father. "Last spring he just barely made the grade. This fall he is on trial, as you might say. If his college work goes well he will stay on the team, but if he fails in his mid-term exams, he will be out on his ear—bingo!"

"Bingo is a game," said Dumpling seriously.

Dorothy got up and began to remove the dishes.

"The worst of it is," said Professor Ridgeway, "he didn't register for something easy as he might have done. He signed up for chemistry, and apparently he's having a fearful time with it."

"I'll say he is," said Dorothy from the kitchen doorway.

"H_2O is chemistry for water," said Dumpling. Everybody looked at her, but nobody thought of anything to say. Then Mother kissed her on the back of the neck. "Too bad you'll never be eligible for football, Dumpling," she said.

"But, Father," said Susan, "how nice that it's chemistry he's having trouble with, because Professor Jones lives right next door, and if you just went over and talked to him—I know he thinks we're noisy and hard on flowers and all that, but he respects *you* very much. If you would just go over and tell him how important it is for Tommy Tucker to stay on the team—"

"And do you think Professor Jones would respect me any longer if I did?" asked Father. "No indeed. What

Tommy does, he must do himself. If we made it either easier or harder for the football players, it would be completely unfair to the other students. What he needs is a good tutor."

" 'A tutor was teaching two tooters to toot,' " remarked George. And he began to play "Tootle—tootle—toot" on an imaginary fife.

But Susan was quite serious and troubled about all this. She went out to the kitchen to help Dorothy with the dishes.

"Is chemistry really very hard, Dorothy? I don't think I'll try it when I get to college," Susan said.

"Of course you will," said Dorothy, "if you want to. Anybody can do anything if she really wants to. I might be milking cows and slopping pigs, not to mention washing dishes, if I hadn't decided I would go to college and get an education."

"But you're washing dishes now," Susan argued.

"I won't always be," said Dorothy. "This is the bottom rung of the ladder. You'll see. I'll be famous and rich and everything else before I get through."

Susan looked at Dorothy, and she thought, "Dorothy would be quite pretty if she didn't braid her yellow hair so skin-tight and look so determined; she's got beautiful blue eyes. But she doesn't seem to know how to have very much fun, or is it fun just to be so very smart, I wonder?"

They continued to do the dishes in silence for a few moments and then Susan said thoughtfully, "Dorothy, would you be able to be a tutor, do you suppose?"

"I could in some subjects," Dorothy said, "*if* I had time. But you don't mean that football boy with the funny name, do you?"

"He's not a boy," Susan said. "He's a quarterback, and if he flunks in chemistry Midwest will lose the rest of the football games. Haven't you any Midwest spirit, Dorothy?"

"Not much," said Dorothy, scouring the sink in a way to produce the greatest possible cleanness in the shortest possible time.

"If you would tutor him in chemistry—" said Susan.

Dorothy put away the dish mop and folded the dish towels. She put the pots and pans very neatly into the cupboard. When Mother was here alone the pan cupboard was always bulging, and the way Mother started to get a meal was to open the pan cupboard and let all the pans rush out until she found the one she wanted, and then she would shut the doors forcibly upon the rest. Since Dorothy had come the cupboards were neat, and preparations for a meal no longer started with a crash of falling pans.

When Dorothy had finished she stood up, put her hands on her hips, and looked at Susan. "Well," she said, "so you want me to tutor him? I suppose you want me to call him up and say, 'Hello, Mr. Tokarynski. I understand that you are failing in chemistry. Since I'm smarter than you are you'd better let me help you.' "

"I see what you mean," Susan said reluctantly. "It would sound kind of queer, but still if you *could*, Dorothy, thousands of people would be grateful to you, maybe millions."

"Humph," said Dorothy, and without even saying good night she went upstairs to her room two steps at a time.

IV

Busy Saturday

Saturday was a beautiful fall day. The sun shone lazily through a faint blue haze. But the Ridgeway children had too much to do to stop and enjoy it.

Susan helped Mother and Dorothy with dishes and beds, while George cleaned his animal cages and Dumpling took care of the canary.

The name of the canary was Peter Pan, but he was called Dickie for short. Dumpling cared for Dickie faithfully. She gave him birdseed and water every day, a bath and clean paper in the bottom of his cage every other day, and on Saturday he had a little sand and a fresh piece of cuttlebone. She never shirked her duties, partly because Dickie had been given to her as her own bird, partly because that was how she earned her salary of ten cents a week.

But in spite of all this Dumpling was not sure that she liked Dickie. He never seemed to remember her from day to day. He fluttered and cheeped and fussed at her when she came near him. But what bothered her most was that he seemed to want to get out of his cage and away. She

looked at the wild birds flying past the window and making plans for their trip South, and then she looked at Dickie,
and she did not feel happy.

It was not so with George's animals. They seemed quite
contented in the screened boxes and crates which George
had made for them. They either sat and munched things and
grew fat, or they chased each other around in a friendly
way. They did not keep trying to get out. Most of them
had never been out of boxes anyway, for they had been
born in boxes over in the biology or the zoology or the
psychology laboratories. George was a frequent visitor to
these scientific laboratories and he managed to stay close
friends with the student assistants in each place. That was
how he happened to have so many guinea pigs, rabbits, and
white rats. George was crazy about animals and birds and
reptiles. He would have enjoyed owning Dickie too, but
Dickie had been given to Dumpling.

After the household tasks had been done, Susan and
Dumpling hurried into their good clothes. They put the
money they had been saving carefully into their purses.
Dumpling had fifty cents or the savings of five weeks; and
Susan, though she earned twenty-five cents a week as well
as the profits from her baby sitting, had only managed to
save the same amount, because she had a great many ex-
penses.

"Don't forget to go downtown after the Child Study
Clinic," called George hopefully as they went out the gate.

"Remember Sunday," he added. He ran around the house and called it out to them again as they went down the street, for fear they had not heard him the first time.

"We won't forget," they called back.

As they went along Dumpling held hard to Susan's hand. "What will they do to me at the Child Study Clinic, Susy?" she said.

"Oh, it will be easy," said Susan. "Putting blocks in holes and doing puzzles."

"I like that," said Dumpling.

"Don't you remember last year?" asked Susan. "It will be something like that but a little harder, because you're a year older."

"A year is a long time," said Dumpling, trying to remember what they had asked her last year.

"It's *not* like going to the doctor or the dentist," Susan reassured her. "They just want to find out what you know at this age, and how smart you are."

"I think I'm pretty smart, don't you, Susan?"

"Well, of course, *I* think so, Dumpling," said Susan, "but then I'm your sister. There's no telling what they'll think over there. They study all kinds of children."

When they reached the clinic a couple of pleasant but learned-looking young ladies took Dumpling by the hand and led her into a little room by herself. Susan glimpsed a small table which held queer-shaped blocks and cards with pictures on them and other things which she vaguely

remembered from her own past, and then the door closed on
Dumpling and her questioners. Susan sat on a bench in the
hall and waited.

Susan began to think ahead and plan what she would buy
for George's birthday when they went downtown. "Fifty
cents," she thought. "It's not enough to buy him a new football. It would buy a box of that delicious kind of chocolate-
covered taffy that is my favorite kind. Of course he'd like
an animal better than anything else, but he has animals.
What kind of an animal could you buy for fifty cents anyway? The chocolate sort of melts off as the taffy gets
softer, and then you can chew and chew on it for a long
time. I might go to the pet store just to see, but Father
thinks we have too many animals anyway. Let's see, in a
fifty-cent box there would be about twenty pieces of the
chocolate-covered taffy, and that would make four pieces
apiece around the family, or maybe he would only pass it
three times and keep the other four for himself because it's
his birthday."

After Susan had decided on the box of candy, she went
and got a magazine out of a rack and read it from cover to
cover. It was a magazine for parents, and Susan was interested for, although she was not a parent, she found that
being a baby sitter is quite similar to being a parent. When
she had finished the magazine, she sat still and waited. The
learned young ladies seemed to be taking an awfully long
time with Dumpling.

"Goodness! I hope she isn't being too dumb!" thought Susan. "I wish they'd hurry, because we've got to get home before the football game."

She took another magazine and looked all through it. Other children came and went with parents or sisters or brothers holding on to their hands. But still Dumpling didn't come. Susan began to fidget and fret. Should she knock on the door and say to the young lady, "Tomorrow is George's birthday, and we're really in an awful hurry to get home before the football game. Can't you be a little easy on her just this time? After all, she's only six."

But before Susan screwed up her courage to do this, the door opened and Dumpling came out. Dumpling looked very calm and collected, but the two young ladies seemed to be in something of a flutter. Susan knew that it was no use asking them how Dumpling had got along, because it was against the rules for them to tell. The results of the tests were written down on record sheets and put away in filing cabinets, but no one outside the clinic, not even the child who was tested, was supposed to know whether he was smart or stupid.

Susan jumped up and took Dumpling's hand, and, because it was getting so late, they hurried out of the building.

"How was it?" Susan asked Dumpling.

"Oh, it was lots of fun," said Dumpling. "I did more puzzles and games and things than you ever saw, Susy. It was just like a party, only no food."

"Oh, my goodness!" cried Susan, "I forgot my purse. Stand right here and wait while I go back."

She ran as fast as she could back to the building, and there was her purse, still lying on the seat beside the magazines. As she picked it up, Susan saw that the two young ladies were still standing there talking to each other.

"It's the most remarkable thing I ever saw," one of them was saying, and the other one said, "A prodigy! A child prodigy!"

All the way downtown on the streetcar, Susan kept turning this over in her mind. She felt sure that they had been talking about Dumpling, and she knew that it was quite exceptional to be a child prodigy, but whether it was good or bad she could not remember. She thought it was good. She looked at Dumpling with new respect.

"Weren't the puzzles hard, honey?" she asked.

"Well, some of them were," said Dumpling, "but those were the last ones. All the first ones were very easy."

Susan felt excited. She didn't say anything to Dumpling, but she thought to herself, "My goodness! If we have a prodigy in the family, it's almost like having a football hero to mow our lawn!" She wondered if George would want to print tickets.

"Where do you want to go to shop, Dumpling darling?" Susan asked respectfully.

"I would like to go to the big dime store, Susy," said

Dumpling. "The one that has pickles and canary birds and plants and lamps and sets of dishes and everything."

"All right," Susan said, "but that's not really a dime store, Dumpling. You know things cost all sorts of prices."

"I call it the dime store," said Dumpling.

"All right," Susan repeated. "So if I leave you there at the dime store and come and collect you again, will it be okay, Dumpling? Because I want to go up to that yummy taffy store, and we haven't much time."

"It will be okay," Dumpling said.

So Susan left Dumpling at the door of the big Woolworth store with instructions to meet her there in fifteen minutes, and she hurried up the street.

Susan thought that even if she were blind she would be able to find the taffy and caramel-corn store, because there was a rich, warm, and bubbling smell that came out of the door and billowed up and down the street. It was the best possible advertisement the store could have, better than an electric sign or a sandwich man walking up and down.

The rich, warm smell reminded Susan that breakfast was long past and that luncheon was still quite far in the future. It would have been very nice to spend part of her money on the beautiful golden-colored caramel-corn for immediate eating, but she kept the thought of George and his birthday resolutely in mind.

"A fifty-cent box of chocolate-covered taffy please," she

said to the clerk with more firmness than appeared to be necessary.

When the box was filled, wrapped, and paid for, she put it under her arm and walked out of the store. A block away from the store Susan made a pleasing discovery. The rich, warm and bubbling smell was still with her, although she had left the store behind. It clung to the box of candy as the fragrance of spring clings to the earliest flowers.

"Smell, Dumpling!" Susan said, holding out the white-wrapped box. Dumpling was waiting for her outside the dime store.

"M-m-m!" said Dumpling. "Good!"

In her hand Dumpling had a little cardboard container with a wire handle. It looked like the kind of container in which one carries pickles or oysters or sauerkraut or ice cream. It might have been any of these things, for the big dime store had practically everything.

"What did you get, honey?" asked Susan.

"Susy, it's a surprise," said Dumpling.

"A surprise for George, I know. But don't you want to tell *me*, Dumpling?"

"No, Susy. It's a surprise."

Going home in the streetcar, Dumpling held the container very carefully. Susan was worried.

"It isn't ice cream, is it, Dumpling?" she asked. "Because today is quite a warm day, and I just thought—"

"No," said Dumpling, "it isn't ice cream, Susy."

Susan's package gave off a very delightful odor, but Dumpling's package had a sound rather than a smell. It had a very, very tiny sound, like something sloshing. "It must be pickles," Susan thought.

The farther along they went, the more crowded the streetcar became. People were already going to the football game. Automobiles with pennants flying kept whizzing by them, and there were other streetcars up ahead. The one they were on moved very slowly.

"Well, I'm glad it's not ice cream," said Susan. She stopped worrying about Dumpling's package and began to wonder how they would be able to get home from the streetcar. The streetcar stopped right by the stadium, and they would be the only two people going against the crowd instead of with it. There was one place where they would have to cross College Avenue, too, and that was bad because a steady stream of cars flowed by on football days.

"I hope there's a policeman," Susan said. "I hope Officer Cahill is there." Officer Cahill was the college policeman, and the children were good friends of his.

V. *How to Cross a Street*

On ordinary days College Avenue was quiet and calm under its big elms. The old houses and the new houses seemed to slumber there in the sunshine, and across the street the University campus was quiet and drowsy, too, with students strolling along in pairs or sitting on the steps of the buildings, studying their lessons.

On football days, however, everything changed. College Avenue suddenly became like the State Fair and the Shrine Circus and the Fourth of July all rolled into one. Almost

Dumpling held tight to Susan's hand. "It's much nicer looking down from the Tower, isn't it, Susy?"

"Yes, it is," said Susan. "Keep watching for Officer Cahill, Dumpling."

Their hats, which were fortunately attached with elastic, were knocked off the backs of their heads. They dodged and pushed and threaded their way through the oncoming crowd.

"Talk about the thundering herd!" said Susan, gasping, as she clutched her box with one hand and Dumpling with the other.

"And the maddening crowd," said Dumpling, holding her little cardboard pail tight against the middle part of her. It was her middle part which stuck out the farthest. The pail had begun to leak a little bit, and even in her anxiety about getting home Susan could not help thinking, "Yes, it must be pickles! I hope George won't be too disappointed."

"Susy, there's a policeman across the street," said Dumpling, "but it's not Officer Cahill." There was a strange policeman in the street. He was a fine, stalwart officer in a blue coat with a whistle in his mouth. But he was not using the whistle, because all of the cars and people wanted to go in the same direction toward the stadium. He had nothing to do but stand quietly by and watch them go, making sure that nobody got into trouble.

Only Susan and Dumpling wanted to go in the opposite direction. They stood on the curb and tried to attract the

everybody in town seemed to be on the way to the footba
game, and those who were not going to the game were ther
to sell something.

"Soov'nirs! Soov'nirs!" shouted the boys with boards fu
of bunches of red and yellow ribbon. Red and yellow wer
the University colors. Fastened to the red and yellow rib
bons were cunning little metal footballs. "Get your soov'
nirs, folks!"

"Popcorn! Peanuts! Soft drinks!" sang the popcorn mer
and the whistles on their wagons made an exciting accom
paniment.

And all up and down the street the auto horns were honk
ing.

"Balloons! Balloons!" other people cried. "Get your bal
loons and release them at the kickoff!"

"Park your car! Park your car! Right here to park you
car!" cried the Gimmick boys, and many other people
and down the street. The only vacant space where cars we
never parked was the space in the Ridgeways' driveway,

"Corsages! Corsages! Get your lady friend a chrysant
mum to pin on her coat!" other people shouted.

"Hawkers and vendors," Susan said wistfully.

Honk! honk! honk! beep! beep! It was into the mid
this hurly-burly that Susan and Dumpling stepped
they got off of the streetcar. And, because they were
home and not to the stadium, they were the only
going in the wrong direction.

officer's attention, so that he could help them get across the street.

"Officer! Officer!" called Susan, but the honking and the beeping, the whistling and the shouting, drowned out her voice completely. She tried again.

"Help! help! Police!"

No result.

"Help, police! Murder!" called Susan, who had read enough of Mother's mystery novels to know how to attract a policeman's attention. "Murder! Murder! Help! Help!"

One or two people stopped to look at them, and a kindly old gentleman said, "Little girls, is anything the matter?"

"Yes," said Susan gratefully. "We are Professor Jonathan Ridgeway's children, and we would like to get across the street."

The old gentleman shook his head. "Too bad," he said. "I'm afraid it can't be done until the crowd is in the stadium."

"But *we* are *Professor Ridgeway's* children," said Susan firmly. Nearly everyone knew and respected her father. Still the people who had stopped to see what was the matter shook their heads. "Too bad," they said. Then Dumpling spoke.

"Tommy Tucker is our friend," said Dumpling in a clear voice, squeezing her leaky package tight against her fattest part. "Tommy Tucker mows our lawn in the summer, and we would like to get across the street."

"You *know* Tommy Tucker?" cried one of the people

who stood around them. He was a young man in a red and yellow striped sweater. "Hey, she says she knows Tommy Tucker!"

"Hey, Tommy Tucker's friends want to get across the street. Officer! Officer! Here's some traffic going the other way!" Everyone around them began to shout to the policeman. He blew his whistle and held up his hand. Brakes screeched and wheels stopped going around.

"Tommy Tucker's friends want to get across the street!"

The policeman came himself to escort them. Everybody nearby who had heard about Tommy's friends began to laugh or applaud. Somebody shouted, "Rah! Rah! Rah! Tommy Tucker! Tommy Tucker's friends!"

A wave of excited cheering rippled up and down the street. Susan and Dumpling walked sedately across the street in front of the honking cars and the impatient people. When they were safely on the other side Susan breathed a long sigh.

"Whew!" she said.

George was hanging on the front gate, watching for them. "My, you're late!" he said. "Lunch is all ready, and Mother is worried about you."

"Well, we're here," said Susan.

"I see you have some packages," George said cordially.

"Oh, the bottom's coming out!" cried Dumpling and she began to run.

"Can I help you?" cried George and Susan in one breath.

"No," said Dumpling, "it's a surprise, but I've got to get a fruit jar quick!"

She disappeared at top speed into the basement.

Susan went into the kitchen where Mother and Dorothy were dishing up luncheon.

"Oh, Mother, what a day!" she cried.

"You poor lamb," said Mother, "I never thought it would take you so long. Did you spend too much time downtown?"

"No, it was the clinic," Susan said. "They took hours, it seemed like. When we got to town we just hurried right along."

"Were there so many other children ahead of Dumpling?"

"No, they took her right in, but they kept her and kept her. And, Mother, do you know what?"

"No. What?"

"I heard them talking afterwards, and Dumpling is a child progidy."

"You mean prodigy?"

"P-r-o-d-i-g-y," spelled Dorothy.

"That's right."

"No," said Mother. "Impossible!"

"It's perfectly true," said Susan. "That isn't bad, is it? It means she's tremendously smart, doesn't it?"

"Yes, yes," said Mother, "but I'm sure there's some mistake, Susan."

"But she really is smart," said Susan. "She knew enough to tell them we were friends of Tommy Tucker's, and then everybody helped and they stopped traffic and let us go right across the street."

Mrs. Ridgeway took the milk and butter out of the refrigerator. "My goodness!" she said. "Where *is* Dumpling?"

"She's gone down to the cellar to put her present in a fruit jar."

"A fruit jar? What did she get?"

"She wouldn't tell me," Susan said, "but the carton it was in leaked. I think it must be pickles."

"Ssh!" said Mother. "Here comes George."

"She wouldn't let me in the laundry room," George said. "She's doing something with water."

"Oh, dear!" said Susan, "she must have dropped them and had to wash them off."

"What's 'them?' " asked George.

"Now, George," said Mother, "you know you don't want to find out until tomorrow, dear. It would spoil all the surprise."

"Don't I?" asked George. He was not sure.

Susan was washing her hands for lunch, and words kept running through her mind. "Progidy—prodigy," murmured Susan.

"P-R-O-D-I-G-Y," spelled Dorothy firmly, and Mother said, "Learn to spell it, Susan, and then forget about it. I'm sure we haven't any such in this family."

"Mother, we're going to miss the kickoff," George said. "It's almost time for the game to begin."

"Well, put your luncheon on trays," said Mother, "and take it to the Tower."

"Oh, a picnic!" they cried, hurrying to get trays.

"Mother, aren't you coming with us?" Susan asked.

"No, thank you, dear. I'm going to do my Saturday baking."

"Can Dorothy come?" asked Susan.

"Yes, of course," said Mother. "Wouldn't you like to take your lunch to the Tower, too, Dorothy, and watch the football game?"

"Football?" said Dorothy. "I've got a lot of studying to do after I'm through with the lunch dishes. Football is just for people who want to kill time."

"How can you kill time?" asked Dumpling.

"With an ax, probably," said George.

"Tut-tut!" said Mother. "You've been at the manuscript of my novel again, George."

"But, Dorothy," said Susan, "honestly you ought to come. It's more fun!"

"I didn't come to college for fun," Dorothy said. "I came for an education, and I've worked like a trooper to get this far. I can't let down now and waste my Saturday afternoons."

The children sighed. There was really nothing you could do about a girl like Dorothy.

Perilously balancing their trays, they climbed the many, many stairs to the Tower. Mother called after them, "Don't disturb my papers, will you?" and then she added the other usual "don't." "Don't lean out too far. I'd hate to have to collect the pieces with the broom and dust pan."

"We won't, Mother," they called back, and George added, "We haven't leaned out too far—yet."

When Mother was working in the Tower they did not enter without knocking. But today the Tower belonged to them. Mother had put the cover on her typewriter and a beautiful green stone, which George had once given her, on top of her papers to keep them from flying out the open window.

Father had a study downstairs where he wrote lectures and articles on such strange and difficult things as "The Cuneiform Signaries or Syllabaries of the Assyro-Babylonians." The young Ridgeways did not try to read Father's papers because his papers were far too learned, but sometimes they read Mother's and made comments or suggestions.

There were many things to do in the Tower besides watching football games. Susan was fond of stories, and the Tower set her imagination to work and made her dreamy. Sometimes she tried to get George to act fairy tales with her.

"Rapunzel! Rapunzel! Let down your long hair," or "Sister Anne! Sister Anne! Do you see anyone coming?"

But George was not very good at fairy tales. He preferred flying kites or throwing out little twists of yellow paper to see the wind take them. He had discovered that the Tower was not quite straight by dropping a long string with a pebble tied to the end of it out of the window and observing that it did not hang even with the walls of the Tower. He had rigged up a windmill arrangement for telling how hard the wind was blowing. George had heard about Galileo and the Leaning Tower of Pisa, and he found it both scientific and amusing to experiment with falling objects and gravity when so many unsuspecting persons were conveniently passing below.

Dumpling usually brought her dolls to the Tower and played house under Mother's desk. "Now, Irene, deary," she would say to her limp and shapeless favorite rag doll, "we are going to have a tea party this afternoon, deary. Call Mrs. Umpty-tumpty and ask her to bring her little children over, will you, deary? Ting-a-ling-a-ling! Is this Mrs. Umpty-tumpty? My mama says—"

"The Tower is really no good to Dumpling," George would say regretfully to Susan. "She could play house under Dad's desk downstairs just as well."

"I know," replied Susan, "but she's happy."

Today when the Ridgeways reached the Tower with their luncheon trays, they found that the crowd in the street below had almost disappeared. The big stadium in the next block was crowded with people.

Only Dean Ambrose was to be seen driving calmly down the street in his shiny blue Studebaker.

"Why is Dean Ambrose always late?" George wondered.

"He never rushes around to find a parking place the way other people do."

"It's because he has a special parking place of his own," Susan said. "You know that little piece of ground between the round corner of the stadium wall and the square corner of the street? The policeman saves it for him, and he always goes in there."

Over in the stadium they could see the red and yellow flags and pennants, and the red and yellow balloons which would be released to float away on the breeze at the moment the game started. They could hear the college band playing the college song, "Forever, Dear Midwest."

Mother had the old portable radio on her desk, and now George turned it on and tuned it to the football game. The music came in loud and sweet, and the excited voice of the commentator said, "The team is coming onto the field now. They're wearing their yellow suits with the big red M's on the jerseys. Here's Tommy Tucker, friends. Tommy Tucker, number twenty-five. Listen to the cheer the crowd is giving him. They sure do love that guy, Tommy Tucker!"

"Oh, boy! Oh, boy!" cried George, gulping his luncheon.

An exciting afternoon was before them.

Tower Seats

The Ridgeway children enjoyed every part of the Saturday afternoon spectacle. They enjoyed the boom of the big gun that was always shot off at the first kick of the football. They enjoyed seeing the red and yellow balloons that people in the stadium had been holding suddenly float upward and drift away on the breeze, like hundreds of red and yellow flowers against the blue field of the October sky.

Part of George's researches in the Tower as to which way the wind was blowing were connected with balloons. He always hoped that some day the wind would be in exactly the right direction, and that all of the red and yellow balloons would come sailing right by the Ridgeways' Tower, some of them directly into the windows. So far this had never happened, but George was always hopeful.

Most of all, the Ridgeways enjoyed the magnificent playing of Tommy Tucker. They took turns watching him through the field glasses, and they cheered and applauded with the crowd. But today the opposing team was a very good one, and even with Tommy Tucker playing it looked for a while as if Midwest might not win. The afternoon was almost over, and the opposing team had a score of 13, while Midwest had only 7. Just at this exciting moment Dorothy came up to the Tower. Even in the midst of their anxiety and suspense the children were surprised to see her. She was carrying a tray with three mugs of milk and a plate of fresh cookies.

"No, I didn't come to see the game," she said briskly. "Your mother's making cookies, and she said you were always hungry again by this time in the afternoon. But how in the world you can be, I don't know."

They laid down the field glasses with whoops of joy and helped themselves to milk and cookies. Dorothy set the empty tray on Mother's desk and took up the field glasses. "I can't imagine how you see a thing from here," she said. "The stadium's a block and a half away."

"Try it and see, Dorothy," said Susan, her mouth full of cooky.

Dorothy adjusted the glasses in a brisk and efficient way and turned them on the stadium. The voice of the commentator came over the radio, "It's thirteen to seven, folks. The score is thirteen to seven in favor of Caronia. Midwest can't seem to wake up today. Tucker doesn't have his usual flash—"

"Worried probably," said Dorothy unfeelingly. "He ought to be!"

"It's Caronia's ball, second and six, on the Midwest forty-two yard line," said the announcer. "They come out of the huddle. T formation. The ball goes to Jorgenson. He's fading back for a pass. He gets it away. It's a long one intended for Smith on the left. The pass is—Great Gulliver! It's intercepted! Number twenty-five came out of nowhere and picked it out of the air! Tommy Tucker's got it! He got away from the Caronia guard! He's up to the thirty-yard line and still going. The forty! Oh boy! Look at him dodge! He's past midfield. He's in the clear, folks! The twenty-five, the fifteen, the ten! He's over! He's over for a touchdown! And was it ever a beauty! That ties up the score and Midwest will try for the extra point."

The Ridgeway children were capering and cheering in a fine spray of flying milk. "Give us the glasses, Dorothy!" they begged. But Dorothy's eyes were glued to the lenses. "Dorothy! Dorothy!" they cried, pulling at her skirt. "We all take turns looking, Dorothy."

Dorothy gave back the field glasses. She drew a deep breath.

"Well," she said, "he might as well go out in a blaze of glory, I s'pose. The poor, dumb kid!"

"Dorothy!" Susan cried, "you're just heartless! I don't see how you *can* be like you are!"

Dorothy collected the empty mugs. "Humph!" she said as she went downstairs with the tray, but somehow the word did not carry its usual scorn, and the sound of it was soon lost in the roar of applause announcing that the Midwest kick for the extra point was good, and that the Midwest team had won the game.

As the crowds came out of the stadium after the game, George led his own cheering section in the Tower.

"Yay! Yay! Yay! Tommy Tucker!"

The passers-by would look up and smile, and sometimes they would join in and cheer, too.

As soon as the parked cars had all been moved out of the Gimmicks' back yard, the Gimmick boys started out to look for objects that had been dropped or lost.

That was another thing that Father would not let the Ridgeway children do; but Tim and Tad usually came over to exhibit what they had found, so George and Susan did not have to die of curiosity.

Susan and George could see the Gimmick boys now, as they moved slowly and carefully all around the outside of the stadium. They poked among the fallen leaves and the discarded line-up programs and empty popcorn boxes. They examined every inch of trampled grass. If one of them leaned over to pick up a treasure, George focused the field glasses on him and cried out to Susan, "He's got something, Susy!"

"What?"

"I can't see. Ten cents maybe, or a beautiful diamond ring most likely."

"Well, if it's a diamond ring, they'll have to turn it in to the Lost and Found Department. They can't keep it," said Susan. She was turning over the pages of Mother's mystery novel to see how it was coming along.

"But they might get a reward," said George hopefully.

"Listen, George," said Susan. She began to read, "*It appeared to be a pure case of accident. The body lay beside the road, and there was a crimson stain of blood upon the snow.*"

"That's a new one, isn't it?" asked George with interest.

"Yes, it is," said Susan. "I believe she's started all over again, and look what a lot she's written! *The Inspector said gruffly, 'Another poor guy blotted out by a hit-and-run driver!' Young Angus McAngus did not say anything, but he stooped quickly and picked up a small object which he slipped into his breast pocket.'*"

"The diamond ring!" cried George.

"No, no," said Susan, "the clue."

"She's got the same amateur detective," said George. "It's good old Angus McAngus."

"I guess it's the same old murder," Susan said, "but she's just writing it another way."

Just then there was a shout from the lawn below, and they looked out to see the Gimmicks with their hands full of loot.

"Look what we got!"

"Wait," shouted George, "we're coming down."

They really did sound like a thundering herd when the

three of them ran down the uncarpeted stairs in a great
hurry. Only the very last flight of stairs was silent. That
was because it had a carpet and also a gently curving banister which was good to slide on. There was even a stopper
on the post at the end of the banister, so that you did not
slide off into emptiness and fall to the floor. The stopper
was a statue of a lady, made of metal. She had one arm up-
raised, holding a lamp, and Susan called her the traffic cop.

The Gimmick boys had not found any diamond rings.
In fact the Ridgeways were not greatly impressed by the
things which the Gimmick boys had found: a half-empty
box of popcorn, a broken balloon, a red button, a streetcar
token, a trampled chrysanthemum, and a bow of red and yellow ribbon without the tiny football.

"Is *that* all?" asked George in amazement.

"Well, it's more than you've got," said Tad. This was
very sadly true.

"How much did you make parking cars?" asked Susan.
Of course she knew already, because the Gimmicks' back
yard would only hold four cars and that made one dollar,
but she wanted to be polite.

"We made one dollar," they cried proudly. "Don't you
wish your father would let you park cars?"

"Well, we have other things," said Susan, trying hard to
think what they were.

"We have Tommy Tucker to mow our lawn," said
George.

"That's just in the summer," said Tim.

"Yesterday too!" cried Susan.

"But not every Saturday like we park cars."

"We have a Tower," said Dumpling in a clear voice. They all looked at her. Suddenly Susan was filled with a warm surge of pride.

"We have something else you haven't got," she said. "Dumpling is a prodigy."

"A which?" asked everybody. Even George and Dumpling were amazed.

"What is a prodigy, Susy?" asked Dumpling in a frightened voice.

"It's something very, very special," Susan said.

"Good or bad?" asked Dumpling.

"Good, I think," said Susan. She began to spell it, "P-R-O-G—no. P-R-O-D-I-G-Y, *prodigy.*"

The Gimmick boys were plainly impressed. "Is it something you catch, like chicken pox, or what?"

"No, it's nothing like that," Susan said, enjoying her superior knowledge. "But the ladies who tested her at the Child Study Clinic were simply amazed about it. 'Did you ever see anything like it in your life?' they said."

"Susy," asked Dumpling anxiously, "what do I do to get to be a prodigy?"

"You have to be very, *very* good—" said Susan. She was going on to say, "very, very good at doing puzzles and matching cards and answering questions," but just at that instant Mother called out the back door, "Susan! telephone! Hurry up, dear, I've been all the way upstairs for you, and I didn't know you were out here."

"Oh, I know what it will be," cried Susan as she ran into the house. "It will be a call to sit with the Terrible Torrences."

The three boys stood and looked at Dumpling after Susan had run into the house.

"Didn't you know," asked George, "that you were that progeny thing, Dumpling?"

"No," Dumpling said.

"Here, Dumpling," said Tim, "you can have the car token."

"Thank you," Dumpling said, putting the token in her pocket.

"You can have the corsage too," said Tad, putting the broken chrysanthemum into her hand.

"Thank you," Dumpling said. They kept looking at her until finally Dumpling went away and crawled under the lilac bush in the corner of the yard. She sat there and thought. "P-R-O-D-I-G-Y," she remembered. "And I had to be very, *very* good. I didn't know I was, but, if I have to be— Yes, I *will* be very, very good."

Susan did not come outdoors again. Mrs. Torrence wanted her to sit that evening, and Mother needed her to lay the knives and forks for dinner.

George and the Gimmicks wandered around the yard,

discussing the football game. Of course the Gimmicks had not seen it, because they did not have a Tower, and they were too busy outside of the stadium, but they had heard about it from the radio and from the people who parked cars in their back yard. They agreed with George that Tommy Tucker had been a great hero.

"But, do you know what?" asked George. "If he doesn't pass his chemistry exam at the mid-term, he'll be taken off the team and not allowed to play."

"No!" cried the Gimmick boys. "Why?"

"Well," said George sadly, "it seems like chemistry comes first, and then football."

"Who says so?" asked Tim angrily.

"It's a rule they have at the University," said George, and he added, nodding his head toward the house next door, "Professor Jones teaches chemistry."

The three boys went and looked over the wall and the hedge from the Ridgeways' back yard, and they could see Professor Jones innocently tying up his late chrysanthemums. The late chrysanthemums were tall and full of buds, but they would not blossom for a couple of weeks. Every fall there was an exciting contest between Professor Jones' late chrysanthemums and the early frost. Would the chrysanthemums bloom before the frost? Or would the frost arrive early and blight Professor Jones' chrysanthemums before he was rewarded with blossoms?

There were two things in life that Professor Jones

enjoyed very much. He enjoyed chemistry and he enjoyed his flower garden. He liked his house on College Avenue because it was near the chemistry building and because it had a fine rich soil surrounding it for a flower garden. The things which Professor Jones did not like were football, children, rabbits, and dogs. This made his life rather difficult, for there was the football stadium "in his lap," as Mother would say, and on each side of him lived children. The Terrible Torrences were always digging holes under his hedge and coming through to pick his flowers or turn on his hose and make a wading pool in the midst of his strawberry bed. The Ridgeway children were well behaved, as children go, but they *did* shout and cheer in very loud voices, and sometimes George's rabbits got loose and came over to eat Professor Jones' delicious tulips and daffodils and parsley. Professor Jones had been heard to say, "We have everything else, but, thank goodness, there are no dogs!"

George cleared his throat. "How did you like the football game, Mr. Jones?" he called.

"Football?" repeated Professor Jones, looking around at them in surprise. "Oh, yes, football. I'd say it was very noisy. Yes, very noisy! Far too much traffic. Something should be done."

"It was a wonderful game," said George, "and you know who won it? Tommy Tucker!"

"Tucker? Tucker?" repeated Professor Jones. "Never heard of the fellow."

"His name is Tokarynski," said George, making a sound like a sneeze, "Thomas Tokarynski. He takes chemistry."

"Ah!" said Professor Jones. He stood up and rubbed his back. "Ah, yes, Tokarynski! A nice young fellow but a terrible chemist. Yes, yes, a terrible chemist."

"Doctor Jones," said George, remembering to use the professor's formal title, "I hope he doesn't flunk in chemistry, because then he couldn't play football any more."

"Well, well," said Professor Jones mildly, "maybe if he didn't play so much football he would be a better chemist."

"Oh, but don't you see?" cried George, gathering all his forces for a tremendous debate. "Don't you see, Doctor Jones—" But just then Mrs. Jones came to the back door of her house and called, "Supper, Jonesy."

"If you will pardon me," said Professor Jones, "it seems imperative that I fill the inner man."

"What did he mean by that?" asked Tad.

"Chow," said George. "He's going to put on the feed bag."

"I guess it's all true," said Tim gloomily. "He said Tommy was a terrible what-you-call-it."

"Chemist," George said. "It doesn't look as if we'd get a bit of help from *him*."

Susan came to the back door of the Ridgeway house. "Soup's on," she shouted.

VII

The Thousand and One Nights

Susan set off for the Torrences with a copy of *The Arabian Nights* under her arm.

"Don't expect to read, dear," Mother said. "It really isn't safe."

"I know, Mother," replied Susan, "I just thought that after they got to sleep, *if* they *do* get to sleep—"

"Well, good luck, dear. And call me if you need help."

"Thank you, Mother."

As Susan went up the Torrences' front walk the Terrible Torrences, in pajamas and bedroom slippers, rushed out at her, uttering blood-curdling cries. They had Indian war bonnets on their heads and tomahawks in their hands. Fortunately the tomahawks were made of cardboard, because the Torrences immediately caught hold of Susan's hair and began trying to scalp her. Susan was used to something like this, and she proceeded calmly up to the Torrences' front door while the two little boys shrieked and howled and danced around her.

"I'm here, Mrs. Torrence," she called from the front hall.

"I'll be right down," said Mrs. Torrence from upstairs.

In a moment Mrs. Torrence floated—or at least seemed to float—down the stairs in a lovely dove-gray evening gown with a crimson rose on the shoulder. Behind her gleamed the white front of Professor Torrence's dress shirt. "We're going to the Saturday night dance, Susan," Mrs. Torrence said. "Can you keep the boys away from us until we get started, so they won't spoil our clothes?"

"I'll try," said Susan, taking a firm hold on the backs of Alvin's and Rudy's pajamas.

"Mama, we want to kiss you good-by," shouted the Terrible Torrences.

"You just kiss Mama's hand tonight, boys," said Professor Torrence. "It's safer that way."

Mrs. Torrence extended a lovely hand, and the boys bestowed several wet and grimy kisses on various parts of it. Susan continued to hold them by the backs of their pajamas, so that they would not swarm all over the lovely dress.

"They're all ready for bed, Susan," Mrs. Torrence said, "*if* you can get them to bed. If you can't—well, just do the best you can with them. I wish you all kinds of luck."

"Thank you," said Susan politely, although she was never quite sure what she had to be thankful for at the Terrible Torrences' house.

"Try not to let them break anything, dear," Mrs. Torrence continued.

"Or leave the faucets running," said Professor Torrence.

"Or put oatmeal into the mailbox."

"Or the cat into the coffee pot."

"I'll try," Susan said without much conviction.

"We do whatever we want to do," said Alvin, and Rudy added, "Yah! Yah! Yah!"

"Oh, dear," said Mrs. Torrence with a long sigh, "they haven't very good manners, but I don't know what to do with them. I honestly don't."

She and her husband hurried away down the walk as if they were escaping from something.

For a moment the young Torrences stood still looking after their fleeing parents. When they were still for a moment they looked quite angelic. Suddenly, for the first time in her life, Susan felt a little sorry for Alvin and Rudy. What if she had heard her own parents admit that they did not know what to do with their children? All the safety and comfort of home would be gone, Susan thought. No, even if parents might sometimes feel that way, she decided, it was better not to say so, because children needed to believe that there was someone at home wiser than they were.

"Yah! Yah! Yah!" shouted the Terrible Torrences, beginning to leap up and down and trying to wriggle from Susan's grip. Susan took a long breath and rallied all her forces.

"Now," said Susan, "let's play a nice quiet game of tiddlywinks, and then, if you are real good, do you know what I'll do? I'll let you go to bed."

This was a good approach, but it did not fool the Torrences.

"We aren't going to bed tonight, not at all," Rudy said, and Alvin said, "Susan, do you want to see something?"

"What is it?" asked Susan cautiously.

"We've got it down in the tool shed at the back of the yard."

"What?"

"Even our mama doesn't know it's there."

"What *is* there?"

"You come and see. Someone lost it at the football game, and we've got it in our tool shed."

"Oh, I see," said Susan, much relieved. "A box of popcorn or a ribbon souvenir, like the Gimmick boys found?"

"No, it's much, much bigger," said Alvin.

"It's alive," said Rudy.

"Alive?" repeated Susan. Her momentary feeling of relief vanished. "And you didn't tell your mama?"

"It's a surprise for her birthday," said Alvin.

"Is her birthday tomorrow? Why, so is George's!" This slipped out before Susan thought.

"Mama's birthday is in January," said Rudy, and Alvin said enthusiastically, "Is George's birthday *tomorrow?*"

"Well, sort of," admitted Susan. Mother had said, "We'll ask the Gimmicks for supper on George's birthday, but it might be just as well if the Torrence boys don't know about it." Now, unfortunately, they knew.

"Are we invited to the party?" asked Rudy.

"There isn't going to be a regular party," said Susan, "just the Gimmick boys for supper."

"We can come too," offered Alvin.

"No," said Susan, "you were invited to Dumpling's party because you're her age, but George is older."

"We ate the candles off Dumpling's cake before they were lighted, didn't we, Rudy?" said Alvin.

"Eskimos eat candles," observed Rudy. "We'll come to George's party too, Susan."

"Oh, no," said Susan.

"Oh, yes!" cried the Terrible Torrences.

Susan tried to think of something to divert their minds. "Didn't you want to show me something?" she asked.

"Come out to the tool shed," they said.

Darkness fell early now in October, but the air was still warm. A full moon shone in the sky. The Terrible Torrences led the way down the back walk to the tool shed with Susan trailing along worriedly at their heels.

"We can't get it out," explained Alvin, "because Rudy lost the tool-shed key after we had locked it in."

"But you can see it through the window," said Rudy.

"What is it?" asked Susan again. She was rather glad to know that whatever they had captured could not get out.

"It's a lion," said Rudy.

"No, a wolf," said Alvin.

"But nobody would bring lions or wolves to a football game," reasoned Susan.

"You just look in and see," the Terrible Torrences said.

As they approached the tool house Susan could hear a noise which was at first like a strange rustling, then a scratching, then a bumping and a stamping. Something seemed to beat against the side of the tool house. Then another noise began which was neither singing nor whining nor yammering, yet partook of the nature of all three. It was almost like moaning, and in the midst of her growing horror Susan could not help thinking that such a sound would be a wonderful one for Mother to describe in her murder-mystery novel.

"Faint in the moonlight," Susan thought, *"gleamed the tool shed in the back yard, and from out of it came the sound of a struggle and then the awful unearthly sound of a moan. When Angus McAngus reached the spot and forced open the bolted door, the corpse had breathed its last."*

The Terrible Torrences climbed up on a box so that they could look in the one small window.

"Yah! Yah! Yah! Wolf!" they cried, banging on the window. The noises from the tool shed became more violent.

"Is there more than one?" asked Susan.

"Just one, but it's big," said Alvin.

Susan peered through the small, dusty window. Inside she could see something enormous and active heaving and leaping about in the darkness. Whatever it was, the corpse had certainly not breathed its last. It was terribly alive.

"Is it a pony?" asked Susan.

"No, no, no!" cried Alvin and Rudy, howling with laughter. "A wolf! A wolf!"

Suddenly the thing stopped leaping about, and in the darkness they could see that it was looking at them. Its two eyes shone green and very strange.

The Terrible Torrences were never afraid of anything, and certainly Susan would not have admitted fear, but now the three of them took hands and fled back up the garden and into the house. The Torrences did not stop running until they had reached their bedroom. They bounded onto their beds and covered their heads with bedclothes.

"It had eyes," said Alvin from under the bedclothes.

"Didn't you know?" asked Susan. But the boys would not say.

Susan sat down between the beds, hoping that Alvin and Rudy would forget and go to sleep while they were buried under the bedclothes. However, this was too much to expect.

With a motion like the eruption of twin volcanoes, the bedclothes suddenly flew up into the air, and the Terrible Torrences appeared again. At once they began beating each other over the head with pillows. One of the pillows ripped at the corner and a gentle snowstorm of white feathers began to fill the air.

"Stop! Stop! Stop!" cried Susan. She shouted it so violently that the two little boys were surprised. Without thinking what they did, they stopped fighting and looked at her.

"What's the matter, Susan?"

"*You* are the matter," said Susan. "Now you lie down in bed quietly, and I will read you a story."

"Oh, blah! blah!" jeered the Terrible Torrences. "Little Red Hen. Little Peter-Peter Rabbit!"

"Those are very good stories," said Susan.

"Yah-yah! Those are stories for babies."

"Well," said Susan, lifting her eyebrows, "and what are you, if I may ask?"

"We are not babies!" cried Alvin.

"*We* are big boys," shouted Rudy.

"Oh, indeed?" said Susan. "Then how come you have to have a baby sitter?"

They looked at her in amazement.

"Because our mama does not dare leave us alone," said Alvin.

"And why doesn't she dare leave you alone?"

"Because we'd get into mischief."

"Then," said Susan with relentless logic, "you are babies. Big boys can be left alone, and they don't get into mischief."

The Terrible Torrences thought this over. "If we didn't have a sitter, you wouldn't have a job."

"Sometimes I wish that I didn't have a job," said Susan. "Or else I wish that there was a real nice *little* baby, a *real* baby, in the neighborhood for me to sit beside."

The Terrible Torrences thought this over too. Finally Alvin said, "Well, we'll listen to a story. But don't read—tell."

Susan's thoughts went scurrying around very quickly. The book she had brought with her was downstairs, but she knew most of the stories by heart. It was all about Scheherazade and the thousand and one nights. In it Scheherazade, the wife of the cruel Sultan, had been condemned by him to death at dawn. But each night she told him such an interesting story, which broke off just at the most exciting point as the day dawned, that the Sultan kept putting off her execution from day to day. She told him stories for a thousand and one nights, and finally the Sultan decided that she was much too valuable to lose, and he promised that she should never be executed but should live happily ever afterward. Susan felt great sympathy for Scheherazade. To tell stories to the cruel Sultan who was plotting her death must have been very much like telling stories to the Terrible Torrences who would not go to sleep.

"All right, boys," said Susan, "I will tell you a story about a man named Ali Baba, and about the forty thieves who had a cave in the mountains."

"Thieves?" cried Alvin, delighted.

"How many is forty?" asked Rudy.

"Oh, a very great many," said Susan. "Well, once upon a time—"

As Susan talked a sense of wonder began to dawn upon

her—for the Terrible Torrences were *listening*. Everyone had tried reading nice stories to the Terrible Torrences, stories about little hens and little pigs and good little boys and girls, and they would never listen. But this was about thieves! Now, for the first time, they were hearing an exciting story told, and they were listening. "Oh, dear," thought Susan to herself as she talked, "I hope I'm doing the right thing."

They listened and they listened, and about nine o'clock their eyes began to grow very heavy. Still listening, they fell back on their untidy pillows, and first Rudy, then Alvin, went soundly off to sleep.

On tiptoe Susan moved about the room, picking up feathers and making things tidy. She drew the covers up to their chins and stood looking at them for a moment before she turned out the light. Anyone who didn't know would have said that they were sleeping angels.

"Just one night," murmured Susan, as she went softly downstairs, "but it certainly seems like a thousand and one."

VIII

Happy Birthday, Dear Georgie!

George's birthday dawned fair and bright. The sun shone on the falling yellow leaves, making them look like bits of floating sunlight.

"Happy birthday, everybody!" cried George, leaping out of bed and looking expectantly under his pillow and under the bed and on all the tables and shelves. There was nothing unusual to be seen, but George's spirits were not dampened. He knew that there would probably be no presents until breakfast time, and perhaps not until after Sunday School, if they were all late and had to hurry.

All through breakfast Susan was busy relating her adventures of the night before. "And after they went to sleep," she said, "I got to thinking about the Thing in the tool house. It hadn't had anything to eat. I got to worrying. I felt sorry for it, but I didn't know would it eat hay or meat or carrots or what. So I went down to see."

"You never did!" everyone cried. "Weren't you scared?"

"No, it was funny, but after I began to feel sorry for it I wasn't scared."

"And was it a wolf, Susy?" asked Dumpling.

"No, of course not."

"But how could you get in to find out?"

"I found I could push the little window open, and there were some meat and vegetable scraps Mrs. Torrence had forgotten to put in the garbage, and I shoved those through the window, and I could hear the Thing chomping them, and then it stood on its hind legs and kissed me."

"Good gracious! Was it human?"

"No, with its tongue. It's a dog—the biggest dog I ever saw in all my life."

"Oh, boy! A dog!" yelled George, *"This I must see."*

"Wait, George, wait," called Mother, as George with toast in one hand and a glass of milk in the other was preparing to dash away to the Torrences.

"Stay here, George," cried Susan. "Santa Claus came last night."

"Oh, is that *so?*" said George, taking his seat again with a self-conscious expression on his face. "Well, that's a mighty funny thing to happen in October."

"Is now the time, Susy?" asked Dumpling, sliding down off her chair.

"Yes, now, honey."

Dumpling, with the morning bib which she wore flapping over her shoulder, hurried away to the basement. Susan departed in one direction, Mother and Father in another.

George was left sitting alone at the breakfast table, gulping his milk and muttering, "Oh boy! Oh boy!"

In a moment they were all back, trying to hide mysterious parcels behind their backs.

"George darling," Mother said, holding her package out, "you might as well open this first. It isn't very exciting but it will be useful."

"Thank you, Mother," cried George, giving her an enthusiastic kiss. It was a small, flat box. "I guess it isn't alive," said George, shaking it gently. He opened it, and it contained a half-dozen pairs of beautiful new socks.

"Oh boy!" said George, "I certainly needed them."

"I know you did, dear," said Mother, "and so did I. I got so tired of darning your old ones!"

Susan thrust her package into George's hand. "Here, George."

George shook it. "It rattles," he said, "but I guess it isn't alive. Thank you, Susy." He unwrapped the paper, and the rich warm smell reached his nose. "Oh boy!" he cried, "it's Susan's favorite candy."

"I thought it might be nice for all of us," Susan said. "You especially though, George."

"Gee! Thanks!"

"Here, George," said Father. Father was beaming with satisfaction and pride.

"Oh boy!" said George. "A book! I bet it's Mr. Ditmar's snakes."

"No, George," said Father, "this is a very special book. I went to every book store in town to get it but with no success. Then I tried the second-hand and the Salvation Army book stores. At the very last place I found it."

"Thanks, Daddy," cried George. Out of the paper wrappings came a very odd looking old brown book. It had had a lot of wear. George spelled out the title on the cover. "*The Young Carthaginian* by G. A. Henty. Well, well, well," said George.

"George," cried Professor Ridgeway happily, "that is the book that first interested me in history. In that book I first heard of Hannibal. I have been following Hannibal and his triumphant armies ever since. Let me read you the first paragraph, George."

"After breakfast, darling," said Mrs Ridgeway to her husband. "Dumpling hasn't given her present yet."

"Excuse me, Dumpling," said Father.

In silence Dumpling set her package before George. It was obviously a fruit jar wrapped in an old comic section.

"I couldn't wrap it very well, Georgie," Dumpling said.

Susan was afraid that George was going to be disappointed. She kept trying to whisper "pickles" into his ear.

"It looks all right, Dumpling," said George. "I like the comic section better than tissue paper. Thank you, Dumpling." As he unwrapped the layers of paper a tiny sound came out of the package. It was a sloshing sound. George's politeness suddenly vanished. "Oh boy! Oh boy! Oh boy!"

he yelped. "It's alive! It's alive!" And, as the last wrapping fell away, he shouted in ecstasy, "Turtles! Oh, look, everybody, Dumpling gave me turtles!"

It was indeed true. Dumpling had given George five small turtles. George was simply wild with delight. He rushed around kissing everybody and then went back to his turtles.

Dumpling did not look as happy as George. "They want to get out into something bigger, George," she said. "I didn't know what to put them in, and I didn't know what to feed them."

"Ant eggs," George said happily, "that's what they eat. We can buy ant eggs in little boxes at the corner drug store, and we'll put the turtles in the old goldfish bowl, Dumpling. Oh boy! Oh boy!"

The turtles were about the size of round silver dollars. Four of them were a dark grayish-green on their backs, but the fifth had been painted with a tiny spray of red roses and the inscription, "Hi Pal!" All five were alike on their undersides, that is, a sort of red and green and white plaid. If you touched them, they drew in their heads and legs and waited. If you left them alone, they all began struggling and trying to get out of the fruit jar.

Dumpling looked very mournful. "They want to get out," she repeated.

"We'll fix that," George cried. He rushed to the attic for the old goldfish bowl. Together he and Dumpling filled the bottom of it with sand and one large rock for climbing and sitting purposes. Then they added water, and one by one the five turtles were introduced to their new home.

"I bought all the turtles they had at the dime store," Dumpling said. "They just had five, and I bought every one."

"Gee! it's wonderful," said George. "One turtle would have been fine, but *five turtles!* Oh boy!"

"George, honey," Mother said. "You must hurry now or you'll be late to Sunday School. The turtles will be here when you get back."

Father put his hand in his pocket. "What is the price of ant eggs, George?"

"Twenty-five cents for the biggest box," said George.

"Buy yourself the biggest box, George, and here is ten cents for the collection at Sunday School because you are ten years old."

All the way to Sunday School George was making delightful plans for the future of the turtles. "I'll build five little tracks side by side, one for each turtle, and then we can race them. Will the Gimmick kids *ever love that!*"

"It won't hurt the turtles to race them, will it?" asked Dumpling anxiously.

"No, they'll love it," said George. "It will give them exercise. They won't have to go any faster than they want to, but we'll see which one gets to the end of the track first. Maybe I'll print up tickets."

Susan was thoughtful on the way to Sunday School. George hadn't even tasted the chocolate-covered taffy yet. She thought, "I believe Dumpling *is* a prodigy. She was the only one of us who knew exactly what George wanted."

Dorothy had gone home for the day to visit her family on the farm, so Susan helped Mother set the table for dinner.

"Mother," Susan said, "did you notice anything about our presents to George this morning?"

"Yes, I did," said Mother, smiling. "Dumpling was the only one who stopped to think what George really wanted. I got George socks because I was tired of darning his old ones, and Dad got George a book that he had enjoyed years ago when he was a boy, and you—"

"Yes," said Susan, "I got my favorite kind of candy. Mother, I think that Dumpling *is* a prodigy."

George was out in the back yard busily constructing five little runways, each one just the proper width for a turtle. Neither Susan nor Mother noticed that Dumpling was in the next room where she could hear every word they said. She was standing by the goldfish bowl looking at the five turtles, and they were *trying to get out!* Behind her glasses tears glittered in Dumpling's blue eyes. She went upstairs to her room and sat very quietly on her bed with Irene clasped in her arms.

It was a very fine birthday for George. After dinner they

drove to South Lake Park to look at the monkeys. Whenever George was allowed to choose an entertainment that was the one he chose.

When they arrived home at five o'clock the Gimmick boys were sitting on the front steps waiting for them. They had been invited to come at six o'clock, but they had not been able to wait that long. They had brought George an almost good, used tire, ready to hang from a limb of the big elm tree in the back yard.

The boys and Professor Ridgeway went to the garage and the basement for a strong rope, a ladder, and everything needed to put the tire swing into immediate use.

Susan and Dumpling helped Mother to get the supper ready and to put the candles on the cake. The sight of the candles made Susan remember the Terrible Torrences. "I hope they don't come," she said. "They said they were going to, but probably they will forget."

"Better put on a couple of extra places then," Mother said with a sigh. "The little Torrence boys will remember."

"Alvin and Rudy have rememberies like elephants," said Dumpling.

The Terrible Torrences arrived promptly at six. Usually they came to the back door and walked in without knocking, but on George's birthday they came to the front door and rang the bell. The Ridgeways and the Gimmicks were just sitting down to supper when the doorbell rang.

"See who it is, please, Susan," said Mrs. Ridgeway, but of course everybody knew.

"We have brought George a present," announced the Terrible Torrences as soon as Susan opened the door. They began to sing,

> "Happy birthday to you,
> Happy birthday to you,
> Happy birthday, dear Georgie,
> Happy birthday to you."

at the same time walking briskly into the dining room, accompanied by their present.

The present was the Thing, which Susan had seen in the tool house. It was almost as big as a pony, and it was something between a Great Dane, a mastiff, and a Saint Bernard. Yes, a dog, but what kind of dog was the puzzle. Its color was yellowish brown with black markings, and it had a long and strong tail that wagged enthusiastically. It was full of kindliness and good humor. It went leaping around the table to greet each and every one of them, its big mouth half open in what was surely a smile of delight.

"George," said the Terrible Torrences, "we have brought you a present. Our mama wouldn't let us keep it, so you can have it for your birthday."

"Oh, quick, look out!" cried Mother in alarm, but before anything could be done the creature's long, strong tail had wagged a cup and saucer right off the table.

"Here is George, Dog," said Alvin, showing the Thing which person he belonged to. "Here is your new master." The dog seemed to understand at once, and he was very pleased to have George for a master. He licked George's cheek, and then he tried to climb into George's lap.

For once in his life George was speechless. Then the "Oh boy! Oh boy's!" began to gurgle out of him. He clasped the large animal affectionately about the neck, and in their mutual pleasure and delight George's chair was overturned, and the two of them rolled and tumbled on the floor.

The Gimmick boys leaped from their places with cheerful shouts; Dumpling stood on her chair and waved a fork; Rudy, in the confusion, ate two candles off the birthday cake; and really it was a very exciting climax to George's birthday.

IX. *An Ad in the Paper*

"Now, of course," said Father sensibly, "someone must own this dog. We shall have to find his owner."

"No dog ever grew as big as that," said Mother, "without someone to feed and care for him."

It was almost bedtime. The Gimmicks and the Terrible Torrences had departed. All of the excitement was over. In the middle of the living-room floor the Dog slept a sleep of happy exhaustion. Occasionally he opened one eye to see if George was still there, and when he saw that he was he wagged his tail against the floor, *wham! wham! wham!* George was exhausted too, but he was full of bliss.

"But if he had owners," George said, "they would be out looking for him. He would have on a collar with a license. I'm sure nobody cares as much for him as we do."

"Still we must advertise in the paper," Father said. "We must also watch the ads. Somebody's probably very unhappy tonight without his dog."

"I can't believe that," George said, "because look how happy *he* is. If he had a good master who loved him, *he* would be unhappy too."

"You keep calling him 'he,' " said Susan. "Haven't you thought of a name?"

"You might call him Tiny," said Mother, beginning to laugh. And then she added more seriously, "How do you think we can feed a dog like this, George? He's eaten everything we have in the house tonight, and I'm sure he isn't full yet."

"I'll find *some* way to feed him," George said stoutly.

"You might start feeding him guinea pigs and white rats," suggested Susan.

Dumpling had been sitting very quietly in her small chair, rocking Irene to sleep. But now she cried out in alarm, "Oh, no, Susy!"

"Honey, I was just joking," Susan said. "We'll buy frozen horsemeat for him at the butcher shop."

"And do you know how much that will cost?" asked Mother. "It will cost almost as much as feeding another member of the family. If I could sell my murder-mystery story maybe we could afford a dog, but the way things are I simply don't see how."

"I know what," cried George, changing the subject with great tact, "we'll call him Angus McAngus!"

"No, no!" said Mother. "Poor Angus is getting along too badly already. Don't use his name in vain, please!"

George looked speculatively at Father, "We might call him Hannibal," he said.

"That's an excellent idea!" said Father enthusiastically, but then he remembered Mother's fears about being able to feed the creature, and he added, "but, of course, there is little use in naming this animal, when we hope so soon to restore him to his rightful owner."

"The Terrible Torrences just called him 'Dog,'" said Susan.

"Why don't you call him Torrible Terence?" asked Dumpling sleepily.

They all stopped and looked at her, and then they cried out, "Well, why not?"

And so, as George was fond of telling people later, "Torrible Terence is named Torrible Terence after the Terrible Torrences." It made a very nice little tongue-twister if spoken rapidly.

After Torrible Terence had been given temporary lodging for the night in the garage, and the guinea pigs, rabbits, and white rats had been locked up, and the canary bird covered, George and Susan and Dumpling came and looked at the five turtles.

"Oh boy," said George, "do I ever have a swell menagerie! A regular zoo! Gee, did I ever have a wonderful birthday!"

"George, they aren't sleeping," said Dumpling. "They want to get out."

"By tomorrow they'll be used to the goldfish bowl," said George cheerfully. He dropped a few ant eggs on the water for the turtles' midnight supper.

"Come, children," Mother said, "you *must* get to bed. Tomorrow is school, and we must put this ad in the paper, and you've had such a busy exciting day."

"Gee, Dumpling," said George, as they went upstairs, "how did you *know* I wanted turtles?"

"She's a very smart little girl," said Susan proudly, "aren't you, Dumpling?" But Dumpling did not say a word. She undressed herself and climbed into bed and pulled the covers up to her chin. Susan and Dumpling shared the same room.

Susan took a much longer time brushing her hair and cleaning her teeth and washing her face than Dumpling had taken, and when Susan crawled into her own bed she thought that Dumpling was asleep.

Susan stretched and yawned and gave a long sigh, and then she promptly went to sleep.

It seemed that she had been asleep for a very long time, when someone snapped on the light beside her bed and Susan awoke with a start. Through a haze of sleep she saw Dumpling standing beside her. Dumpling looked strange without her glasses and with her pigtails all sticking up the wrong way. "Susy," she said, "I wanted to tell you something."

"What is it?" Susan murmured sleepily.

"I would *like* to be very, very good, Susy, like you said, but I don't think I am."

"Well, dear me," said Susan. "But, yes, you *are* good, Dumpling, because you are the only one in the family who thought what George would really like for his birthday."

"That's the trouble, Susy," said Dumpling. She looked quite sad and worried. "I didn't think about George either, not any more than anyone else in the family. I just saw the turtles and they wanted to get out, and I knew I would have to buy them to give them a better place to live."

"Well, for goodness sake!" said Susan. She sat up and

put her arm around Dumpling's shoulder. "And now they're living in the goldfish bowl, honey."

"Yes," said Dumpling sadly, "but, Susy, they still want to get out."

"Never mind," said Susan. "Tomorrow we'll see that George puts them into something bigger."

"You don't think it was bad of me because I didn't think what George would want?"

"No," said Susan. "You pleased him better than anyone else, unless it was the Terrible Torrences."

"But I don't guess I'm very, very good, Susan. Maybe the lady was wrong," said Dumpling hopefully.

"You suit me just the way you are, Dumpling," Susan said, giving Dumpling a kiss on the end of her nose.

"Then I will go back to sleep," said Dumpling gravely. Susan could hear her feet go *pat-pat-pat* across the bare floor to her bed. "Anyway, I aren't terrible like the Torrences, are I, Susy?"

"*I* think that you are very, *very* good," said Susan.

Dumpling climbed into bed with a long sigh, and whether it was a sigh of pleasure or of regret Susan could not tell.

After Dumpling had gone to sleep, Susan still lay awake, thinking. She was more impressed than ever with this child prodigy that they had.

"My goodness!" she said to herself. "Dumpling has a grown-up conscience."

Before they left for school in the morning, the Ridgeway children helped compose an ad for the paper.

Found: Very large brown and black dog near football sta-dium. Owner may call College 2395. Please hurry.

The "please hurry" had originally been "please do not hurry" and had been suggested by George, but just then Terence had wagged an ash tray off a table and broken it into fifteen pieces, so Mother had hastily scratched out the "do not."

They read the Lost ads in the morning paper very carefully, but no one seemed to have lost a dog.

"Hooray!" said George, and Susan added, "Three cheers and a rah!" because there was something about Terence which you could not help liking. Even Mother noticed it, although she tried not to. "He means well," she said, "but he's just at the awkward age."

When Terence heard the kind tone of voice in which she said these words, he came and put both front paws on her knees and began to pull up one of his hind legs with the idea of sitting in her lap. Mother pushed him down and stood up very quickly. "But I *won't* have him sitting in my lap," she added.

"Keep him in today, Mother," George begged, "so he won't get away."

"I'll keep him in until you have gone to school," Mother

said, "so he won't make a nuisance of himself there. But after that I shall let him do what he likes. If he has a home, he had better return to it."

So it was quite an anxious day for George. But when he came home at noon Torrible Terence was lying in the sunshine on the front porch, lazily scratching his ear; and when he came home in the afternoon Terence had made himself a nest of leaves in the side yard. Terence seemed to have settled right down and decided to stay. As soon as he saw George he leaped up with yelps of delight, kissed George on both cheeks in the manner of a French general, and nearly knocked him over. For a few moments they wrestled together in the friendliest manner, and then they settled down to business and went to look at the turtles.

The day after a birthday is often more satisfactory than the birthday itself. George wore a pair of his new socks, he passed the delicious chocolate-covered taffy, he looked at the very strange old-fashioned illustrations in *The Young Carthaginian*, he tried out the new swing, and he and Torrible Terence were very, very busy with the turtles.

First of all the turtles had to have a larger place to live in so that they would feel at home and not try to get out. Next George wanted to finish the turtle race track, because he had an idea. The idea was connected both with the turtles and with the problem of feeding Terence.

Terence was interested in the turtles as George was interested in the monkeys at South Lake Park. He liked to

Family Grandstand

go and look at them, with his long ears pricked forward and his nose twitching. Sometimes he would push the goldfish bowl gently with his nose.

"He feels sorry, too," said Dumpling, "because they want to get out."

George went through the pan cupboard until he found an old dishpan which Mother felt that she could spare. Then he and Dumpling put sand in the bottom of it. They added five nice flat rocks, one for each turtle, so that there would be no crowding, and then they poured fresh water around the rocks and sprinkled a few ant eggs enticingly here and there. After that the turtles were introduced to their new home.

"What are you going to call the turtles, George?" asked Dumpling.

Susan thought it would be nice to name them after the Dionne Quintuplets, but George said, no, he would have to take a little time to think the matter over. While he was thinking, he went out and hammered away at his turtle race track.

"Why are you in such a hurry to get it done, George?" asked Susan.

"Because," said George, and added mysteriously, "You wait and see."

Of course the Gimmicks and the Terrible Torrences came to watch too. The Gimmicks were full of helpful and constructive ideas about the proper way to build a turtle track, but unfortunately the Terrible Torrences wanted to help. They snatched the hammer and nails out of George's hands and began to put everything together crookedly and upside down and higgledy-piggledy.

"Hey, you quit that!" George shouted.

"We can do anything we want to," said Alvin, flinging a handful of nails into the air and kicking boards in every direction, and Rudy shouted, "Yah! Yah! Yah!"

"You go on home now," cried George, "and leave my things alone."

"If we go home now, we'll take our dog."

"He won't go with you."

"We'll make him. We found him first."

"But you gave him to me for my birthday."

"That was yesterday. Yah! Yah! Yah!"

It looked very much as if George was doubling up his fists to punch the Terrible Torrences' noses.

Susan began to speak, quite rapidly, but in a very clear, strong voice, "Once upon a time there was a terrible old man with a very long blue beard, and his name was Bluebeard, and whenever he got tired of one of his wives he killed her and hung her up by her hair in a little upstairs room in his castle—"

In just a moment the Terrible Torrences were sitting one on either side of Susan, as close as they could get.

"Go on," said Alvin.

"What next?" said Rudy.

Astonished but relieved, George undoubled his lists, picked up his nails, assembled his boards, and went on building his turtle track. Susan kept the story going until the turtle track was finished. "And so," she concluded, "the lady's brothers arrived and put an end to Bluebeard."

"Why?" asked Alvin.

"Because he was such a very bad old man," said Susan. "Bad people always have to be punished."

"Why?" asked Rudy.

"Well," said Susan, "I don't know why, but they do. It is much better to get along nicely with other people than to be bad."

"Tell some more, Susan," said Alvin.

"Not now," Susan said, "but I will some other time."

She looked around and she saw that Tim and Tad and Dumpling had been listening too, and even George, at the same time that he had been building.

Susan got up and brushed off her dress and walked into the house. She walked with a new feeling of importance, for she was the only one in the neighborhood, perhaps in the world, who knew how to control the Terrible Torrences.

X

Tutor for Tommy

Susan climbed the stairs to the Tower and knocked on the door. Today the typewriter was not going *clickety-clack*. Mother called, "Come in."

"Mother," Susan said, "I think I know now why you like to write mystery stories."

"Do you?" asked Mother, looking up from her piles of yellow paper. "I'm glad you do, Susy, because sometimes I wonder myself."

"When you tell a story and everybody listens and pays attention it's quite a good feeling," said Susan, "isn't it?"

"Yes, it is," said Mother, "and I suppose that that is one of the reasons I try to write. But the sad part of it is that no one reads or listens. I just write."

"*We* read your stories on Saturday afternoons, Mother, and *we* like them."

"Bless you for that," said Mother. "You are very satis-factory children."

"And when the editor that Mrs. Ewing knows comes to

town, he'll want to make your story into a book, and then everyone will read it, Mother."

"Well, that's what I used to tell myself, Susy," said Mother, "but the time is getting short, and I'm stuck."

"Stuck, Mother?"

"Stuck at chapter nineteen," said Mother. She looked tired and discouraged. She ran her hands through her short, dark, curly hair and sighed.

"Don't you know how it's coming out?" asked Susan.

"No, I don't," said Mother. "I thought that I did, but it won't work that way. A murder mystery is like a jigsaw puzzle, all the pieces have to fit just perfectly, and suddenly mine seems to be a mess."

"Can't Angus McAngus work it out?"

"Confidentially, Susan," Mother said, "Angus McAngus isn't one bit smarter than I am. That's the whole sad story."

"What is happening in the story now?" Susan asked.

"Someone has murdered the Countess's husband," Mother said.

"Was he quite unpleasant?" Susan asked.

"Oh, yes," Mother said, "a perfect wretch."

"That's good," Susan said, "because one never ought to let pleasant people be murdered."

"Certainly not!" said Mother. "And besides," she went on, "the Countess's diamond necklace has been stolen."

"And doesn't Angus know who did all of this, Mother?"

"He suspects the Countess's wicked brother-in-law,"

Mother said, "but the trouble is that all of the readers will suspect the brother-in-law too. That's why I'm stuck. At this rate Angus McAngus is not going to be a bit smarter than any of the people who will read the story. I need a deeper mystery, Susan, and a surprise at the end. Can you help me?"

"I'll think about it, Mother," Susan said gravely.

"Let's go downstairs," Mother said more cheerfully, "and make cookies. That birthday cake vanished into thin air."

"And Aladdin rubbed his wonderful lamp," said Susan dreamily, "and the birthday cake vanished into thin air."

"Also," said Mother on the way downstairs, "I need another corpse, another murder, but not an ordinary one at all. This must be something very strange and extraordinary, because we are dealing with no ordinary criminal."

"Mother, I thought about Angus McAngus and the criminals the other night when the Torrences took me to look at the dog in the tool shed. It made a wonderful noise like a kind of moaning. If you could only describe that, Mother, and the moonlight, and the thumping noises, and the mysteriousness of everything!"

"Yes, yes," said Mother. "Now let me see, peanut-butter cookies, chocolate-chip cookies, which will be quicker?"

"We might ask George," suggested Susan. "I think he would be quite good at plotting murders."

George was at work on the kitchen table, printing tickets

with his rubber-stamp set. The Gimmicks and the Torrences had left, because it is not so interesting to watch a person print tickets as to watch him build a turtle track or to listen to Bluebeard. Terence was asleep at George's feet, and Dumpling and Irene were playing house under Father's desk. Dorothy had a book propped up in front of her so that she could read with her eyes while she peeled potatoes with her hands.

"George," Susan said, "can you help Mother think up a real unusual murder for Angus McAngus to solve?"

"Well," said George, continuing to print tickets, "there might be this horrible old scientist in the zoology laboratory who cut up all kinds of frogs and things, and one day Angus McAngus came in and there was the scientist in a bottle, pickled in alcohol."

"My goodness!" said Susan. "Who done it?"

"The frogs," said George.

"That is a little too unusual," Mother said. "Would you mind moving to the other end of the table, George, so that I can get at the flour bin?"

"Mother," Susan said, "you might have a baby sitter—"

"Oh, yes," cried George enthusiastically. "And in the morning the parents would find two little corpses in their cribs, and that would be the end of the Terrible Torrences, only Angus McAngus wouldn't have any trouble finding Susan because all the clues would point—"

"George!" cried Mother. "How can you be so horrible!"

"I was just trying to help."

"I know, dear, but you have such ghoulish thoughts. I guess I'd better work this out myself."

"Mother, will you make a lot of money when you sell your mystery story?"

"*If* I finish it, *if* I sell it," Mother said, "I might make something. We could certainly use some extra money in this family."

"If you sell your mystery novel, Mother," cried George, "will we be able to buy all the horsemeat Terence wants to eat?"

"I expect so," Mother said, "but long before I finish it, I hope that his former owner will claim him."

"The evening paper!" cried George and Susan together. They dashed out to the front porch, and the evening paper was lying there waiting for them. Terence dashed out after them, as if he understood how vitally he was concerned.

George and Susan sat down side by side on the top step and slowly opened the paper to the classified advertising section. Terence sat beside them with his front feet in George's lap and his tail going *wham! wham! wham!* on the porch floor.

Susan ran her finger up and down the Lost and Found columns. She read out in an impressive voice:

" 'Found: Very large brown and black dog near football

stadium. Owner may call College two-three-nine-five. Please hurry.' Look, George, there it is! That's us. We've burst into print!"

"But how about the Lost?" asked George anxiously.

"Lost—a watch," mumbled Susan, hastily reading the ads, "a bracelet, a Siamese kitten, a wallet at the corner of Main and Walnut, a light-brown top coat, a—a—a—*no dogs!*" she cried at the top of her voice. "No dogs!"

"Hooray," cried George, "no dogs!"

Mother and Dumpling both came to the door.

"No dogs?" asked Mother, a shade of regret in her voice.

"*No dogs!*" cried George, and Dumpling waved Irene in the air and cried, "Three cheers and a rah!"

But just then the telephone rang. "George, you had better go," said Mother. "This is your affair."

George went to the telephone. "Hello," he said, "hello, hello, hello. Yes, this is College two-three-nine-five. Yes, we have a brown and black dog. Yes. Yes, we think he got lost in the football crowd. Yes—"

Mother, Susan, and Dumpling came and stood around George and the telephone. Even Dorothy stopped reading and began to look interested. Terence sat at George's feet, looking eagerly into George's face, and his tail went *wham! wham! wham!* on the floor. George's face was very grave.

"Yes—yes—yes—" continued George, and then his face began to brighten. "No," George said, "no—no—no—" He held the telephone against his chest and said, "Mother, Terence isn't a Pekingese, is he?"

"Good gracious, no!" cried Mother. "Here, let me have the telephone." She spoke for a few moments with the person at the other end of the line, and then she said, "But this is a very, very large animal. Largeness is one of his distinguishing features. Well, I'm terribly sorry. I do hope you find your Pekingese. If we see him, we'll be sure to let you know." She hung up the telephone.

"Mother!" they cried, "Mother! It wasn't for Terence after all!"

They all began to laugh and shout and hug each other, even Mother, and Terence went wild with delight. He knocked three ornaments off a shelf with his tail, but only one broke, and nobody scolded him.

While they were in this pleasant frame of mind a knock sounded at the back door. Their happy faces fell again.

"We didn't give our *address* in the ad, did we?" cried George.

"No," Susan said, "I'm sure we didn't."

They followed Mother to the back door and stood behind her apprehensively as she opened it.

"Well, Tommy Tucker!" Mother exclaimed. "It's certainly nice to see you! Come right in."

"Hi, Tommy! Tommy Tucker!" cried the young Ridgeways, happy once more.

"We thought you were someone who had come to take

our dog," cried George. And after that they had to intro-
duce Torrible Terence and relate to Tommy all the events
of George's birthday.

Mother went on making cookies as calm as you please
while the great football hero, Tommy Tucker, sat on a com-
mon kitchen chair and patted Terence's head and listened to
the things the children had to tell. He seemed to be very
much interested, but he was quiet. Susan thought that he
looked worried. Dorothy kept right on studying and peeling vegetables without even being polite enough to look
around.

Mother put a pan of cookies into the oven, and then she
smiled at him. "Tommy," she said, "they will wear your
ears off talking. Maybe you had something to say yourself."

"No," said Tommy. "I like to hear these kids talk. I've
got brothers and sisters at home about like them; and you
don't exactly look like my mother, Mrs. Ridgeway, but
your doughnuts have the same flavor. I guess that's why I
came here today. I don't know any other reason."

"You played a good game on Saturday, Tommy,"
Mother said. "You were wonderful."

"Wonderful, Tommy!" cried the children.

"Oh, were you at the game?"

"No, I was baking," Mrs. Ridgeway said. "We run
through baked things just the way you run with a football,
Tommy. But I listened on the radio, and they all told me—
why, even Dorothy—"

"Humph!" said Dorothy, clearing her throat.

"Well, it's all over now," Tommy said, "even the shouting."

"I can't believe that," Mrs. Ridgeway said. "What ails you, Tommy?"

"Mid-terms come next week, and I'm dumb."

"That's what Dorothy said," remarked Dumpling.

"But we wouldn't believe her," George said fiercely.

"It isn't true, Tommy! Really it isn't!" begged Susan.

Tommy was silent for a moment and then he said gloomily, "All this hero stuff, it really gets me down. Everybody shouting and cheering for me—it ought to make me happy. Maybe it would if I was as good as they say I am. But I'm not. I'm going to flunk in chemistry, Mrs. Ridgeway, and they'll take me off the team, and then—and then—"

"Then they won't cheer any more," said Mother calmly.

"Mother!" cried the children reproachfully.

"That's right," Tommy said, "and maybe that's what's bothering me. I don't know. But I think I feel worst because I'm so dumb I can let a thing like chemistry lick me."

"You sound so sure that you are licked, Tommy," Mother said. "Why is that?"

"Well, mid-terms are here, and honestly I can't remember a blessed thing. I study this crazy stuff half the night, and when I wake up in the morning it's all gone."

Dorothy turned around and entered the conversation. She waved a carrot in one hand and a paring knife in the other. Her blue eyes flashed, and while Susan was angry with her for being so cruel and unkind about football players, still she couldn't help thinking that Dorothy looked very pretty.

"The trouble with you," Dorothy said to Tommy, "is that you don't pay attention. I've seen you there in class, drawing diagrams of football plays right while the professor's talking."

"Well, I don't understand it all. I'm dumb," Tommy said doggedly.

"That's what Dorothy *said*," chirped Dumpling.

"You are *not* dumb," Dorothy said angrily. "Well, I did think you were at first. But a fellow who can learn football the smart way you play it—well, it seems like he isn't *entirely* dumb."

"Dorothy!" cried the Ridgeways in happy surprise.

"The trouble is," went on Dorothy in a tumble of angry words, "you don't know how to study. When an idea seems hard you just lie down and let it walk over you. That's not the way you play football, you know. When you're carrying the ball, and you don't see any way through the line, you go right ahead, dodging and pushing and smashing through. You make the touchdown. You aren't afraid. But when it comes to chemistry you're afraid. You let the line stop you. Someone should have taught you how to study, big boy, away back in high school!"

"Well, gosh! I guess no one did," said Tommy humbly.

"Then someone ought to now!"

"Who's going to?"

"You could get a tutor," Susan said thoughtfully.

" 'Two tutors were teaching two tooters to toot,' " said George.

"Dorothy could tutor you," Susan said. "Couldn't you, Dorothy?"

Mother looked at Susan and Dorothy and Tommy. Suddenly she began to smile. "Susan is right," she said. "I believe Dorothy would be the very one to tutor Tommy. Susan and I will do Dorothy's dishes tonight, and, Dorothy, you can help Tommy study his chemistry while you are reviewing your own."

"Is that an order?" Dorothy asked. "Because doing dishes is a lot easier than teaching a big lunk like this to think for himself."

"It's an order," Mother said firmly.

"That would be fine," Tommy said. "I could come over right after training table. But I *am* dumb, and if she doesn't want to—"

"Of course she wants to! Don't you, Dorothy?" cried Susan.

"Okay," Dorothy said, "I'll do it. But the first thing you've got to do, you've got to stop saying how dumb you are, and get your mind to moving."

"Okay," said Tommy obediently. "Right after supper then I'll be here."

The Ridgeway children shouted with delight. It seemed as if Dorothy might be going to turn out well after all.

That evening Dorothy and Tommy and the children all sat around the dining-room table with chemistry books and notebooks open. Dumpling and George sat on either side of Tommy as close as they could get, admiring him very much. Susan sat opposite, also admiring him. Dorothy sat at the end of the table like a schoolmarm, and if she admired Tommy, you could not notice it.

"Well, the first thing you have to learn," said Dorothy severely, "is how to organize things. Your notebook is a mess. So first we'll go through mine and try to improve yours. And then we'll go back over the last few weeks' work and find out what it is you don't understand."

Mrs. Ridgeway came to the door and looked at them. "Time for bed, children," she said.

"Oh, Mother!" they cried. It was very hard for them to go to bed while Tommy Tucker was in the house. But Tommy grinned at them and tousled Dumpling's hair and made sparring motions at George.

"I'll be here tomorrow night too," he said, "if Dorothy will teach me."

XI

Leaping Lizard

It was beautiful Indian summer weather in Midwest City, and day followed perfect day with no change for the worse. Terence settled down and made himself at home, as if he had always been the Ridgeways' dog, and nobody called up or advertised for him. Tommy Tucker came every evening and studied with Dorothy. The children thought that Dorothy was unkind because she scolded Tommy and told him how poor his work was. But it did seem to be worth while, because Tommy began to give the right answers to her questions, and he made his notebook look a great deal neater and more correct. He began to get his experiments done on time in the laboratory, too, Dorothy said.

There was only one thing that was not perfect in these beautiful Indian summer days: the turtles still *wanted to get out!* George gave them plenty of exercise too, because now his turtle tracks were finished, and he could have turtle races. For one cent George sold a ticket which entitled the purchaser to race one turtle one time. The person whose turtle won the race had his ticket money refunded. In that way

George made four cents on each race. George advertised his turtle races at school, and many of the boys were interested. After school for a few days the Ridgeways' back yard was full of boys, not only the Gimmicks and the Terrible Torrences, but all the boys from school who were interested in turtles. George hoped that he would earn enough money in this way to buy food for Terence.

The first day he collected twenty cents, and he felt that it would be a simple matter to provide for Terence and at the same time have fun. But unfortunately it turned out that the boys had spent most of their pennies on that first day. On the second day George took in two pennies, a kite string, a red crayon, a chipped agate marble, and a lot of promises of future payment. After that the turtle-racing business rapidly declined. There was neither enough interest nor enough money to keep it going.

Dumpling had always been on hand to see that the turtles were not mistreated, and she was glad to observe that the turtles enjoyed racing. As soon as they were set down in the narrow tracks, the turtles began to hurry away as fast as they could go, straight ahead, as if they had a definite destination in mind. After four or five races it would seem that they might have become tired. But this was never so. Back in their roomy and well-appointed dish pan, instead of sitting calmly on the five rocks to rest, the turtles immediately rushed away to try to climb the sides of the pan.

"Oh, George!" cried Dumpling in despair. "They want to get out!"

"Well, Dumpling," George said, "we'll get the big zinc washtub."

So George and Dumpling carried the washtub up from the basement to the back yard. They went to the vacant lot on the back street for all sorts of interesting and unusual stones and a pail of sand. They added a little moss and a few tufts of grass. They used the hose to fill the bottom of the washtub with water. Susan helped them build a twig bridge from one of the big stones to another, and in the attic she found a little Japanese pagoda that they set up on the central stone. It was a lovely thing to see when they had finished with it, and George said confidently, "Now they'll be satisfied." Even Dumpling could not think of anything else to add to the turtles' comfort. So they moved the turtles to their new home and watched them swimming around, exploring it.

Just then the Gimmick boys called over the back fence, "Come and look what *we* got!" So the Ridgeway children ran to see.

The Ridgeway yard and the Gimmick yard followed much the same pattern. Each had a fine wide driveway which swung into an ample turnabout before a carriage house. The Ridgeways used their carriage house for the family car, for garden tools, and for various projects of the children's. But the Gimmick carriage house was the heart and center of Mr. Gimmick's repair business, and in the back yard he collected spare parts instead of grass and flowers. The driveway and turnabout provided the space that the Gimmick boys used for parking cars on football Saturdays, and all around the edge of this space Mr. Gimmick piled spare parts that might come in handy some day in repairing cars for other people. There were old tires, wheels, crankcases, steering wheels, bolts, nuts, monkey wrenches, screws, bits of garden hose, bicycle parts, old lawn mowers, and even a picture frame or two that must have come there by mistake, since one cannot be expected to hang pictures in automobiles.

Today, standing in the turnabout, was a most unusual car. The Ridgeways had never seen it there before. It was a very old and rickety car of a bygone age.

"It's a jalopy," said Tim proudly.

"What's a *jalopy?*" asked George.

"Well," said Tad, "a jalopy is this." So they looked and they knew what a jalopy was.

Some previous owner, with a brush, some red paint, and a humorous turn of mind, had painted signs all over the jalopy. One said, "Shake well before using"; another said, "Must be a screw loose somewhere"; another said, "Rattle his bones, Over the stones." On the back of the car was painted its name: "Leaping Lizard."

"Where did you get it?" asked Susan.

"Pop took it in on a trade," said Tim. "And he says we can play in it, if we don't touch the brakes."

The children swarmed into the old car. Somehow George found himself behind the steering wheel. "Why can't we touch the brakes?" he asked.

"There's something wrong with them," Tim said. "If you pull the hand brake, they lock and you can't move the thing forward or back. You'd have to take it up and carry it to get it out of here."

"Aren't the brakes on now?"

"No. Pop worked a whole day to get 'em disengaged, and he says whoever pulls the hand brake will get the works."

"What are the works?" asked Dumpling. "Is it something to do with brakes?"

"Ya," said Tim. "Pop breaks you in two."

"I see," said Dumpling.

Mr. Gimmick had the appearance of a man who meant what he said, so George kept his hand off the brake. But the children knew how to have fun in a car without using brakes. George made a very good driver, for he could imitate almost all the sounds of starting, stopping, and the different speeds of locomotion. To sit behind George in a jalopy was exactly like taking a nice ride except for a lack of motion.

"Shall we go on a picnic?" asked Susan.

"All right," agreed Dumpling, "but we haven't any food."

"We can play food," Susan said, "just as well as we can play riding."

"How can you *play* food?" asked the Gimmick boys in surprise.

"Here," said Susan, "hold out your hand. I'm giving you a great big bun with a roasted wiener in it. Be careful you don't drop it, and if you care for mustard just open the bun and I'll dab a little in."

Susan had such a way of making things seem real that before he knew it Tad was opening an imaginary bun and holding it out for imaginary mustard.

"I'll take chorc'late cake for mine," said Tim.

"Just a minute, please," Susan said, "while I put the cover on the mustard jar and cut the cake. Here's a real big piece for you now, Tim, and don't wipe the frosting off on your trousers because it's real, real thick and gooey."

"Um-yum!" said Tim, smacking his lips. "Chorc'late cake!"

Somehow with George driving and Susan serving lunch, the Gimmick boys enjoyed their jalopy much more than they would have all alone.

"Susan," said Tad, "the next time there's a football game, you know what we're going to do?"

"Park cars?" asked Susan enviously.

"Oh, sure," said Tim, "but we're going to make money another way too."

"We're going to sell *real* food," said Tad.

"Chorc'late cake?" asked Dumpling.

"No. Popcorn," said Tim. "Our Ma is going to help us pop it. We've already got the bags."

"Bags with red and yellow stripes," said Tad, "like Midwest colors."

"How much a bag?" asked George gloomily.

"Ten cents," said Tim. "You want to order some? We'll save a bag for you if you do—"

"No, thank you," said Susan politely. "We haven't any money."

"We need to make money instead of spend it," said George. "We've got to buy food for Terence."

"Well, look!" howled the Gimmicks. "You haven't any money, but you've got room for four cars to park in your driveway and turnabout. *Why* don't your pop let you park cars?"

The Ridgeway children were silent. They knew from experience that there was no use trying to explain to the Gimmicks about "academic dignity."

Tim ran into the house to get the new signs they had made for the next football game. The signs were of cardboard and were shaped like hands with pointing fingers. One said:

PARK 25¢

Perhaps because she felt envious, Susan was a little bit critical. "You've got the cents sign wrong," she said.

"What you mean we've got the sense wrong?" asked Tim. "It says 'Park,' don't it? That's all it's got to say."

On the other sign they had printed:

PUPCORN 10¢

"And you've spelled popcorn wrong, too," Susan said. "You've got it pupcorn like dog food."

"Dog food!" said George. "Terence!" He gave a long and wistful sigh.

When the Ridgeway children went home, just as a matter of scientific curiosity, just to *see*, George got a yardstick and measured the driveway and turnabout.

"Four and a half," George said. "Yes, four and a half cars we could park. That would be one dollar and twelve and a half cents."

"But who would ever let us park half a car?" wondered Susan.

"Who would ever let us park *any* cars?" returned George. "If it's only playlike, we might as well use all the space we've got."

"Like playing food," said Dumpling.

"We must think," said Susan. "There must be some way."

"Father," Susan said at dinner, "what if the Dean *liked* to see professors' children parking cars? Did you ever think of that?"

"The issue is closed," said Professor Ridgeway firmly.

"The Dean is a reasonable man," said Mother unexpectedly, "at least a reasonably reasonable man, and he's a pushover for football."

"I thought it was a touchdown instead of a pushover," said Dumpling.

"It is true that the Dean is interested in football," Father said, "but I know that academic dignity would come first, especially as a quality in his professors and their children."

"My goodness!" Mother said. "I can remember Pinkie Ambrose—"

"Dean Ambrose," said Father.

"—before he was a dean," Mother said. "He was a substitute guard on the football team when I was in college, and he took it very seriously."

"That's what I mean," said Father. "The Dean is a serious man. He takes everything very seriously."

"I see," said Dumpling.

"Daddy, if George and I would just go to him," suggested Susan, "and explain that the salary he gives you is not very big for five people, and that we could easily stretch it by parking cars on football days, and that we need the extra money because we have a very large dog to feed—"

"No!" said Father. "Forget it, Susan. Turn the dial to another station."

"It was just an idea, Daddy," said Susan meekly.

"Oh, the affliction of living next block to a football

stadium!" Father said. "And another thing: I am reminded of the fact that Halloween and the Homecoming Eve celebration fall on one and the same night this year. I want you to strip the back yard of anything that might be carried away. Garbage cans, clothes lines, wagons, anything you value had better be carried into the cellar or locked up in the carriage house on that night. The back yard must be absolutely empty. Have I made myself quite clear?"

"Yes, Daddy," said Susan and George, but Dumpling had a worrisome thought. "What will the Gimmicks do?" she wondered.

However, the thought of Halloween and the Homecoming bonfire occurring on one and the same night was so delightful that it drove out any worries connected with the state of the Gimmick's back yard or the sad fact that professors' children were too refined to park cars.

"Halloween and Homecoming!" George yelped eagerly. "Oh boy! Oh boy! Oh boy!"

Of all the football games of the season the Homecoming game was the best. It was a time when students who had graduated from the University came home to visit. The houses where students lived were all decorated for the occasion and prizes were given for the best and most original decorations. There was usually a parade with floats and the college band. On the night before the Homecoming football game there was a big bonfire on the practice field with speeches and cheering and much excitement.

For several days before the bonfire students went around collecting fuel. They took old boxes and broken down fences and everything they could find that was no longer useful and that would make a good blaze. Sometimes, of course, they made mistakes and took things which were still useful, if they saw them lying around. Halloween is a great time for making mistakes about other people's property, too, and that was what Father had in mind when he said that the back yard must be cleared of things that could be carried away.

The Ridgeway children always enjoyed Homecoming very much. They saved old wooden boxes all during the year, and when the time came they hauled them up to the practice field in George's wagon. It was exciting to see their own boxes perched high up on the pile of things that would blaze on Homecoming Eve. They always decorated the Tower in honor of Homecoming, too, but they had never won a prize. From year to year the children kept strips of red and yellow tissue paper and a red pennant with a yellow M on it to hang out of the windows of the Tower. Last year, when the Homecoming game was with Michigan, Susan had made a football suit for Dumpling's rag doll Irene, and they had hung her out of the window by her neck with a sign that said HANG MICHIGAN! pinned to her. But Dumpling said that Irene had complained all year of a pain in her neck, and she would not let George and Susan have her for Homecoming again.

"All right, honey," Susan said. "We'll think of something else this year."

"Halloween and Homecoming!" George said happily. "We'll think of something good. This will be the best Homecoming yet!"

"It will," said Susan gravely, "if Tommy Tucker plays in the game. If he doesn't—"

They went and stood around Dorothy as she was gathering up the dishes. "Dorothy, do you think Tommy will play in the Homecoming game, Dorothy?"

"That's two weeks off yet, isn't it?" Dorothy said. "He's got to take his mid-terms before that, and anything can happen. Anything at all! Now am-scray, kids. I'm busy."

XII. *A Turtle Picnic*

Dumpling stood beside the big zinc washtub looking mournfully at the turtles. They were not sitting happily on their rocks nor swimming peacefully around in the water: they were *trying to get out.*

"Oh, George," said Dumpling sadly, "the turtles are *trying to get out!*"

George was beginning to be a little tired of moving the turtles. They seemed more ungrateful and dissatisfied than any well-brought up turtles should be. But George liked to see everybody happy, including Dumpling and turtles, so he said, "Well, Dumpling, there is only one bigger place to put them that I can think of, and that is the bathtub."

"I'll help you put them there, George," Dumpling said.

Mother's typewriter was going *clickety-clack* in the Tower. Father and Dorothy were at the University, and Susan was taking her music lesson. So there was nobody to ask unless they bothered Mother, and George and Dumpling were too polite to do that.

"We'll just have to go ahead and move them without permission, I guess," George said.

It was quite a task to move all of the rocks and the sand and the moss and tufts of grass and the Japanese pagoda upstairs to the bathtub. George and Dumpling and Terence made at least five trips up and downstairs carrying the wet and dripping housekeeping arrangements of the turtles. Terence was not really much help, but he galloped along very enthusiastically. He kept wanting to carry a turtle or two in his mouth, but George said, "No, Terence. You mean well, but you are big and they are little. Somebody might get hurt."

"Not me!" Terence seemed to say, wagging his long, strong tail and looking fondly at the turtles.

But at last the turtles were all moved and installed in the bathtub where they had lots of room. "Of course," George said sensibly, "when anyone wants to take a bath, we'll have to move them. But then we can put them back again. It will give them a change of scene. They'll be happy now."

"You think so, George?" asked Dumpling.

"Sure," George said, "of course!"

Just then they heard Susan coming home from her music lesson, and they dashed down to greet her.

"I got two gold stars on my lesson this week," Susan said. "And I have a new piece, 'The March of the Hobgoblins.' That will be good for Halloween, George, won't it?"

George and Dumpling thought that it would, and they sat on the piano bench on either side of Susan to hear her practice the new piece. Terence sat beside the piano and wagged his tail, *wham! wham! wham!* It almost seemed as if he were keeping time with the hobgoblins' marching. The piece was quite a noisy one, requiring the use of the loud pedal, and there was something about the sound of a loud piece played on the piano that also made Terence want to sing. Presently he added his voice to the music, "Who-o-o-o-o—"

The children and Terence were so interested and were making so much noise that they did not hear Professor Ridgeway come home from the University, put his books and papers on his desk, and go upstairs. It had been a warm day for October, and Professor Ridgeway was hot and tired. He thought to himself, "Now for a bath! A fresh cool tub, some clean clothes, and I'll be a new man."

He went into the bedroom and began to undress in a leisurely way. He was thinking over the very good lecture which he had just given on "Magna Charta and the Emancipation of the Humble Man," and he was feeling very happy. A good lecture just given, a good bath in prospect! He began to hum a tune. Unfortunately Terence's singing, "Who-o-o-o-o—" came up through the floor from the room below and drowned out Professor Ridgeway's happy humming.

It is too bad, Father said to himself, that Terence cannot be taught to howl in the right key. I should say, offhand, that the piece Susan is playing is in C sharp major, but Terence is certainly howling in B flat minor. A great pity— a great pity! But as I just said in my very good lecture, "The rights of the individual are sacred, et cetera, et cetera—"

Professor Ridgeway, thinking eagerly of his bath in a nice clean tub, did not bother to hunt up his bathrobe and slippers, but wrapped a large bath towel around his middle and went into the bathroom. The light from the window was shining in his eyes, and he did not look into the tub, because he knew that Mother always kept it nice and clean, so he just stepped in and reached up to turn on the shower.

Suddenly above the noise of "The March of the Hob-goblins" and Terence's howling and whamming, the Ridge-way children heard a terrible shout.

Susan stopped playing. "It's Daddy!" she cried. "Something awful has happened to him!" The children ran upstairs from the living room. Mother ran downstairs from the Tower.

"What is it? What is it?" they cried in alarm.

Father was dancing about the bathroom, dressed only in his towel.

"Who put these intolerably obnoxious crustaceans into my tub?" he roared. "Who put these—who put these—" Even *big* words failed him.

"Daddy," George said, "they aren't crustaceans. Crustaceans are shellfish; turtles are chelonians."

"George," cried Father, "did you put these—these abominable chelonians into my bath?"

"They wanted to get out, Daddy," Dumpling said.

"Daddy," George said, "we didn't know you were going to take a bath. We planned to take them out in plenty of time."

Dumpling looked over the side of the tub. She said in despair, "They *still* want to get out!"

"Oh, they do, do they?" cried Father. "Well, *I* want to get in. But I won't get *in* until they're *out*, and that's final!"

"Be calm, dear," said Mother. "The turtles have become a problem. We have a problem on our hands."

"All right! All right!" Professor Ridgeway said. "So we have a problem on our hands. But I won't have it in my bath. Have I made myself quite clear?"

"Yes, Daddy," everybody said.

Although Susan had not helped to put the turtles and all their rocks, grass, sand, pagodas, and so forth, into the tub, she was kind enough to help George and Dumpling remove everything and put it all back in the washtub in the back yard.

But quite a bit of sand got away from them and went down the drain pipe, and the next day the plumber had to come.

By dinnertime Father had overcome his desire to have a bath. He was dressed in clean clothes and he was grave and serious.

"Father, we are very sorry this had to happen," George said.

"I want you all to come here and sit down and let me tell you something," Father said.

George and Susan sat on the floor at Professor Ridgeway's feet, and Dumpling climbed upon his lap.

"Daddy," Dumpling said, "the poor little turtles wanted to get out."

"That is the five-millionth time you have said that, Dumpling," cried George in exasperation. "I'm getting tired of it."

"Let Father talk," said Susan. "He's got something to tell us."

"Thank you, Susan," said Father. "Now it's like this: Turtles are wanderers. They don't care about a home. The fact is, as you can plainly see, they carry their homes with them on their backs. If something frightens them and they want protection, they just draw in heads and legs and there they are, safe at home. The same thing is true when they wish to sleep. They don't need a goldfish bowl or a dishpan or a washtub or a—a"—here he seemed to be swallowing a mild sensation of seasickness—"or a bathtub."

"But," said Susan, "if they weren't enclosed in something, Daddy, they would all go away."

"We are reaching the crux of the matter," said Professor Ridgeway.

"A crux is what Grandpa had when he broke his leg," said Dumpling.

"That was a crutch," corrected George.

"Go on, Father," said Susan.

"My proposal is this," continued Father: "that we behave to these turtles in the most humane way possible and let them go where they are obviously longing to go."

"But, Daddy," cried George, "my birthday present!"

"I know, George," said Father. "But imagine yourself in prison somewhere. Would you wish to be detained against your will?"

Dumpling's face had been growing more and more radiant as the conversation progressed. "You mean," she said, "let the turtles go where they want to go?"

"That was my idea," said Father.

"But what would they do in winter?" asked Susan practically.

Of course George knew the answer to that. "They bury themselves in the sand at the bottom of a lake," he said, "and hibernate like bears."

"You see?" said Professor Ridgeway. "And we have no lake bigger than the bathtub, and sand is very bad for the plumbing."

"We could take them to South Lake Park," said George. He thought of the turtles hibernating at the bottom of South Lake with a distinct feeling of relief. "*That* ought to be big enough for them!" he said.

"Oh, goody!" cried Dumpling. "When can we go?"

"I was just thinking," Mother said, "that we ought to have one more picnic before this pleasant autumn weather is gone."

"A picnic!" everybody cried. Terence barked, and Dumpling shouted, "A *turtle* picnic!"

"We could go tomorrow," Mother said, "as soon as school is out and Daddy and Dorothy get home from the University."

"Me?" said Dorothy. "On a *turtle* picnic? Humph!"

But still Dorothy seemed to have as nice a time as any-body on the picnic, and she ate as many wiener buns as George did.

There were fireplaces beside South Lake where they could roast wieners and marshmallows and heat cocoa, and there was nothing much nicer than a picnic at South Lake Park. The only sad part of this picnic was saying good-by to the turtles. Everyone was sad except the turtles and possibly Dorothy and Father, who kept remembering the bathtub. So finally the time for parting came.

When the Ridgeways had all eaten well, and the turtles had been given a final treat of raw beef and all the ant eggs they were interested in, George took the five turtles to the edge of the lake and let them go. The rest of the Ridgeways stood and watched with mixed emotions. Five small turtle heads were raised as if they sniffed the air, and then, with speed, just as if they were racing in turtle tracks, the turtles began to waddle away toward the water. Hi Pal! was the last, and even after he was in the lake, swimming blissfully, he turned his head and looked at them as if to say, "Good-by" and "Thanks for everything." George was touched. Too late he wondered if it wouldn't be possible to hire a boat and collect them all again and return them to the bathtub. But Father said, "No," and Mother voiced the feelings of the others when she said, "They'll be happier this way— and so will we."

On the way home in the car Dumpling took hold of Susan's hand. George and Father were singing,

> " 'Twas Friday night when we set sail,
> And our ship not far from the land—"

Mother and Dorothy were talking about what they had better bake tomorrow.

Susan squeezed Dumpling's hand.

"Susy," Dumpling asked, "do you think that we were very, very good to let the turtles go?"

"Yes, I think so, Dumpling," Susan said.

"Very, *very* good?" insisted Dumpling.

"Yes, very, *very* good," said Susan.

When they reached home Tommy Tucker was there for his lesson, and Susan and George helped Mother unpack and wash the picnic things so that Dorothy could begin at once to teach him.

Only Dumpling went away by herself. She went and stood in front of Dickie's cage and looked at him. At sight of her, the canary got off his swing and began to flutter and leap about, uttering cheeps and twitters of alarm. He never could or would get used to her. Dumpling stood a long time in silent contemplation, and the more she looked at Dickie, the more thoughtful she became.

XIII

A Ghostly Idea

It was while Susan was "sitting" with the Terrible Torrences that she got her idea for decorating the Tower.

"Tell us a story, Susy-Susy-Susan!" cried the Terrible Torrences. "Tell us a horrible, terrible story with lots of blood."

"I will tell you about a girl named Alice who went to Wonderland," suggested Susan.

"No! No! No!" cried the Terrible Torrences. "That's all about little rabbits and getting big and little. We want a horrible, terrible story."

"I can tell you about Hopalong Cassidy," said Susan.

"No! No! No!" they cried. "That's on the radio. You tell, Susan!"

"Well," said Susan, thinking rapidly, "Halloween was coming, and there were two little boys who decided to dress up in sheets and go out pretending that they were ghosts."

"What were the two little boys' names, Susan?" Alvin asked, and Rudy said, "Their names were Rudy and Alvin, weren't they, Susan?"

"Yes," said Susan, "the two little boys were named Rudy and Alvin, and they were invited out to a Halloween party."

"Will there be candles on the cake?" asked Alvin, and Rudy said, "Eskimos eat candles."

"Rudy and Alvin were very nice little boys," continued Susan.

"Oh, Susan, make them *bad* little boys," begged the Terrible Torrences.

"No," Susan said firmly. "They were very *nice* little boys, and brave too, and please don't interrupt so much or you'll never find out what happened to them."

"All right, Susan," said Alvin, cuddling down in bed, and Rudy said, "Tell!"

"Well, because they were so nice, people loved to ask these little boys to parties, and because they were so nice, their mother was just delighted to let them have her best sheets to dress up in, and so Rudy and Alvin dressed up in sheets, like ghosts."

"Like this," said Alvin, pulling the sheet up over his head; and, pulling the sheet over *his* head, too, Rudy cried, "Look, Susan, no eyes."

"And so," said Susan, "these little boys started off to the Halloween party on Halloween night, and it was very dark, and the wind went *woo-oo! woo-oo!* but they were brave and they were not afraid. When they had gone about a block, ahead of them they saw a great big terrible black cat with green eyes. And everyone else was afraid of the cat and ran away, but Alvin and Rudy were not afraid and they went right on."

"*We* were not afraid!" the Terrible Torrences said.

"And when the terrible cat saw two white ghosts coming who were not afraid, the cat made her tail and her back all arched and bristly, and she jumped sideways on her stiff legs, and then she ran away, *clippety-clippety-clap!* And Alvin and Rudy went along to the party. And when they had gone another block, what do you think they saw?"

"A witch!" cried Alvin, and Rudy said, "Susan, they saw a witch!"

"Yes," said Susan. "She was riding around on her broomstick by the light of the moon, and she was having quite a lot of fun, because it must be very great fun to ride a broomstick."

"We ride broomsticks," Alvin said.

"Yes," said Susan, "but only on the ground. This was in the air."

"But they were not afraid, Susan, were they?" said Rudy, "because they were very nice—I mean bad little boys, weren't they, Susan?"

"These little boys were very *nice* little boys," said Susan firmly, "and when the witch saw them she screamed: 'Ghosteses! Oh, my stars and garters! Ghosteses!' And because the two little ghosts were not afraid of her she made her broomstick go high, high, high, *whooshity-whoosh!*

whoosh! And she went far away where there were other people she could frighten. So Alvin and Rudy went along to the party."

"And, when they had gone another block, Susan," said Alvin, "what did they see?"

"Well," said Susan, "in the next block they had to pass a very, very old cemetery, and sitting on five of the very oldest graves were five little ghosts waiting for someone to come by so they could haunt them."

"Were Rudy and Alvin afraid?" asked the Terrible Torrences uncertainly.

"Of course not," Susan said, "not the least bit. So the five little ghosts came all around Rudy and Alvin, and they poked them and felt of them. 'Ghosteses!' the little ghosts said, 'just like us! Hello, brothers.' But Rudy and Alvin said, 'We are Rudy and Alvin.' And all the little ghosts laughed, and when they laughed it sounded like *oo-oo-oo-oo*, very sad and mournful. And one of the ghosts said, 'These ghosteses are not made of mist, they are made of sheet.' And another said, 'When they laugh, it sounds ha-ha-ha! not oo-oo-oo!' And another said, 'They are only pretending to be ghosteses. We will have to punish them!' "

"But Rudy and Alvin were not afraid," said Alvin, "were they, Susan?"

"No, indeed," said Susan. "They saw that the real ghosts were very thin and frail and all made of nothing but mist, and so Rudy and Alvin began to *huff* and *puff*, and *puff* and *huff*—"

"Just like the big bad wolf, Susan?"

"They *huffed* and they *puffed*," Susan said. "And before the five ghosts could do a thing to punish Alvin and Rudy for pretending to be ghosts, Alvin and Rudy had blown the thin, misty ghosts all away, so that they just dissolved like smoke, and there was the moon shining through again, and Alvin and Rudy went on to the Halloween party, and they had a wonderful time."

"And they ate all the candles off the cake, didn't they, Susan?" said Rudy.

"No," said Susan, "they were much too kind and polite to do a thing like that. They just ate cake and candy and cocoa and whatever the lady who was giving the party passed to them, and they didn't grab or snatch."

"No candles," Rudy said, and Alvin, who had been wondering, said, "Why were there *five* ghosts, Susan?"

"I don't know," Susan said. "I just said five, I guess. There are five windows in our Tower."

It was after the Terrible Torrences, looking like angels, had fallen asleep that Susan thought, "Five ghosts, five windows in our Tower. A sheet like a ghost hanging out of each window. A sign that says, *Midwest Makes Ghosts of Its Enemies*. That's it! It will combine Halloween with Homecoming! George will like it."

They began right away, the next afternoon after school, to make the five ghosts to hang out of the Tower windows, because, of course, George was enthusiastic. Dumpling was pleased too. "Now, Irene honey," she said to her rag doll, "you won't have to worry about a pain in your neck."

First of all they had to persuade Mother to let them borrow five sheets.

"Five?" Mother said. "But there are only three of you. Or have I forgotten how to count noses?"

"It's not for us to *wear*, Mother," Susan explained. "We want to decorate the Tower for Homecoming. We want to hang a sheet out of each window, and we'll be very careful of them."

"But won't it look as if we take in laundry or something?" Mother said. "I'm sure Father would think that Dean Ambrose would think that professors' children should not hang their laundry out of the window on football days."

"Mother," Susan explained patiently, "we're going to make the sheets look like ghosts, not laundry."

"Very well," Mother said. "In the attic you'll find some old, clean sheets that are piled up waiting until I finish my mystery novel and have time to mend them. Treat them with gentle, loving care. And *don't* fall out of the Tower window!"

Susan said, "We will" to the first, and George said, "We won't" to the second, and they dashed away to the attic.

Next they collected five wire coat hangers, some drawing

paper, scissors, and colored crayons, and, spreading everything out on the floor of George's room, they set to work.
Terence wanted to help too, and he put his feet on the drawing paper and picked up the crayons in his mouth and
whammed the coat hangers off the bed with his tail. But, in
spite of all this helpfulness, Susan and George made good
progress with their idea.

They drew and cut from the drawing paper five life-sized
ghost faces. Dumpling, who was watching, with Irene
clasped tightly in her arms, asked, "Do ghosts have faces?"

Susan and George stopped working and looked at her.
Then they looked at each other. "*Do* ghosts have faces,
Susan?" George asked, worried.

"*Ours* do," Susan said firmly. So they went on working.
"But we must make them have ghostly expressions," Susan
continued, "with mouths open or turned down at the corners, and eyes rolled up in anguish, and all that sort of thing.
And we must not put in red cheeks, but just leave the paper
white except for terrible mouths and burning eyes."

"How do you burn eyes, Susy?" Dumpling wanted to
know. And Susan said, "Honey, why don't you and Terence
and Irene just go and play house somewhere and let George
and me work?"

After a good many trials Susan and George finally made
five ghostly faces that were horrible enough to suit them.

Then they folded the sheets around the coat hangers in
such a way that the hook of the hanger would be at the back

and would serve as a means of hanging the ghost out of the window. In front of this they pinned the ghost face with a corner of the sheet draped around it like a hood. The five ghosts looked very real and very terrible when they were finished, and Susan and George were pleased. "What shall we do with them until Homecoming?" George asked.

"We can hang them up at the back of the hall closet on the five hooks that we use in winter for our heavy coats," Susan said.

Nobody stopped to think what a shock it might be to Father when he came home and hung up his hat in the hall closet to be confronted with a row of five ghosts with burning eyes. "Chelonians in my bath!" he cried. "Ghosts in my closet! What is a poor man to do in a house like this?"

But the children all came around him to show him that they loved him. Susan and George each took a hand, and Dumpling caught hold of his jacket from behind, and Terence jumped up and kissed his nose from in front.

"Come, Daddy darling," they said, "Mother's got fresh doughnuts!" So away they all went to the kitchen, singing,

> " 'Twas Friday night when we set sail,
>   And our ship not far from the land—"

XIV

Free as the Air

For more than a month now the birds had been gathering in the trees, in great twittering flocks, and then winging away toward the south. Dumpling had watched them with interest and anxiety. They had a long journey ahead of them, but they knew the way, and before winter came they would all be gone. Time was running along very swiftly, and already there were only a few birds left.

Everyday as Dumpling fed and cared for Dickie she thought of this. She thought of the turtles too, and how joyously they had gone swimming away to live their own lives.

"Dickie is my bird," Dumpling said to herself. "I can do anything I want to with him. I would like him to be happy." Dickie shook his wings at her and scolded. He fluttered and cheeped. It seemed to Dumpling that he could not be very happy in his cage or he would behave better than he did.

"I will let him out," Dumpling said to herself, "while there is still time for him to go south with all the rest of the birds."

No one happened to be around when Dumpling reached this tremendous decision, but having made up her mind,

Dumpling acted quickly. She climbed on a chair and un-hooked Dickie's cage from the bracket which held it. Carry-ing it firmly against that part of her which stuck out farthest, she went through the front door and around the side yard behind the carriage house. There was a tree growing there that any bird should enjoy. Dumpling set the cage on the ground and unfastened the clips that attached the top of the cage to the bottom. In the mornings when she changed the paper on the floor of the cage, she had always been careful not to let Dickie escape; but now she deliberately turned the cage on its side with the bottom of it wide open.

Dickie stopped his nervous fluttering and cheeping. He looked at her as much as to say, "For goodness sake! Do you really mean it?" Dumpling made a little shooing motion with her hands. There was an instant's pause, and then with a rush of yellow wings Dickie was out and away. Dumpling followed his movements for a few moments with her eyes, but the tree was full of yellow leaves, and Dickie's yellow wings were soon lost to sight. Dumpling left the cage lying where she had first set it down. She felt satisfied. "I am a P-R-O-D-D-D—one of those things. I am very, very, good," she said to herself.

Dumpling returned to the house and climbed the stairs to her room. She took her rag doll, Irene, out of the wastebasket which made a nice place to park her when she was not in use; and, sitting down on the bed, Dumpling cradled Irene in her arms. Irene never struggled and tried to get away.

Irene was happy and comforting. Dumpling recited a poem she had learned.

> "The world is so full of a number of things,
> I'm sure we should all be as happy as kings.
> Robert Louis Stevenson."

And Irene smiled at her with a painted rag smile that turned up the corners of her painted mouth.

Dumpling was still happy and contented when she came down to dinner. She climbed into her chair and shoved her neatly folded bib onto the floor. "I would like a napkin, please," she said.

"Well, of course, honey," Mother said, "you're getting too big for a bib, aren't you? Get Dumpling a napkin, will you please, Susan?"

"Bib," mused Professor Ridgeway, "a word derived from the Latin verb *bibere*, meaning to drink, sip, tipple."

"*Bibo, bibere, bibi*," said Dorothy; and Susan added, "*Hic, haec, hoc, huius, huius, huius!*" which was the only Latin she knew.

"That would make a good football yell," said George. "*Hic! Haec! Hoc!* Tucker! Tucker! Tucker!"

"How about, *Huius, huius, huius*, we make our rivals fuius?" asked Susan.

"What means *fuius?*" asked Dumpling.

"It means furious, of course," said Susan, "but I want it to rhyme with *huius*."

Just then George glanced up from his Irish stew with real dumplings in it to the spot where Dickie's cage usually hung. Something was wrong there. He was still thinking about football yells and how good Irish stew with dumplings could be as Mother cooked it; but his eyes opened wider in surprise, and another thought began to seep into his mind. When he had managed to swallow his mouthful of stew, he asked, "Where's Dickie?"

The others looked then too, and Susan cried, "The cage is gone!"

There were all sorts of wild speculations.

"The Gimmicks cat!"

"But it wouldn't eat the cage!"

"The Terrible Torrences!"

"But they never did a thing as bad as stealing a canary!"

It was quite awhile before anyone heard Dumpling's small voice saying, "Dickie wanted to get out. I let him. He's gone, like the turtles."

They looked at her aghast. "Dickie!" they cried.

"But he's *always* been in a cage," wailed George. "He wouldn't know what to do."

"He knew to fly," said Dumpling.

"But winter's coming," George said. "Will he know to go South? He hasn't any friends. Will he know to go South all alone?"

"I thought he would know like the turtles," Dumpling said. "He wanted to get out."

Everybody looked at Dumpling, and only George could think of anything to say. "I don't *believe* he wanted to get out," George cried. "It's just the way he acts. You might have given him to me, if you didn't want him, Dumpling. I liked him. I would have fed him—"

"I was thinking about Dickie's feelings," Dumpling said sorrowfully.

"You never think about *my* feelings," cried George.

"George, dear—" began Mother.

But George had reached the boiling point. "Dumpling is not so wonderful after all," he cried. "She gave me a birthday present, and then she made such a fuss about they wanted to get out that we let them out. And now she's gone and let out the canary bird, the only, only bird we had in our zoo."

Suddenly George began to cry, and that surprised the others very much. George had not cried in public since he was Dumpling's age.

"Dear me!" said Professor Ridgeway in alarm. "But, George, Dickie is free; he has his liberty. Liberty is the crown and glory of life, George. If Dickie has found true liberty we must all rejoice. We must imagine him winging his way in sunlight through the trees, wafted by the winds of heaven, singing his sweet song high in the sky of blue—"

"George, dear," Mother said, "there's butterscotch pudding for dessert."

George's sobs grew less violent. Finally he ate two

helpings of butterscotch pudding, but his mouth did not turn up at the corners.

"It isn't just letting things *out*, Dumpling," he said. "You have to think. Will it be good for them?"

Dumpling thought, and she was not as pleased with herself as she had been. Because she wished to be kind to animals, she found that she had been unkind to George, perhaps even to Dickie, who would not know how to protect himself as the turtles had known.

After supper the children went out behind the carriage house and looked around. There was the yellow tree, and there Dickie's empty cage, but Dickie had gone. And no sound of birdnote or flutter of wings came from the branches above them. They had not thought until now how much they really liked Dickie.

"It is almost November," Susan said. "I think the other birds have all gone South."

"Dickie has gone South too, Susy," Dumpling said with more confidence than she really felt.

George was unusually silent and he still had teary splotches on his face. Terence sat close beside George as if he understood that George was sad. He looked up into the trees, too, because the children did, but Terence did not know what he was looking for.

"We might as well take the cage indoors," Susan said. "Perhaps someone will give us a canary bird again sometime, and we will need a place to keep it."

"No!" George said. "You leave the cage there, Susy. It's his home. If Dickie should come back, looking for a place he knows, he'd find his cage waiting."

"All right, George," Susan said. But she thought, "Poor George! I think it would be easier for all of our feelings if we took the cage in and forgot about Dickie."

"Susy," Dumpling said, as they went slowly back to the house, "I was trying to be very, very good, Susy."

"I know, Dumpling," Susan said sadly, "but maybe you shouldn't try so very, very hard."

In the house Tommy Tucker and Dorothy were working at Tommy's chemistry. There was no football game that weekend so they had extra time to work. Mid-term exams started on Monday.

"Tommy, do you think you'll be able to play in the Homecoming game?" asked Susan anxiously.

"I hope," said Tommy.

Dorothy said, "Now, am-scray, kids. The duffer's got to work."

"He isn't a duffer, he's a quarterback, Dorothy," Susan corrected politely. But Dorothy rarely took time to be polite.

"He's a duffer to me," she said, "until he learns his chemistry. Now, scram!"

The Ridgeway children went quietly to bed. Tonight they had unusual anxieties on their minds. Will Dickie know enough to go South all by himself? Will Tommy Tucker be able to crash the mid-term line? Will formula $K_2Cr_2O_7$ throw him for a fifty-yard loss? What are his chances for making a touchdown in chemistry? Will the wind seem very cold in the bare branches of the winter trees? When one is used to birdseed and water in little cups, how will one find food in the gray November woods? And will the Home-coming game be played without Tommy Tucker?

They tried to remember that Halloween and Homecoming fell on the same night and were only a week away. But even that thought did not cheer them, unless they could be sure that Tommy would be allowed to play.

When Mother came up later to see that they were all properly covered and asleep, she noticed that George had not succeeded in washing all the tear stains off his face. She stood still and looked down at George, and she was sorry because the loss of Dickie had made George unhappy. As she looked she became aware of a kind of heaving and wallowing motion along the bedclothes at the foot of the bed. Something large seemed to be moving around there. Then a familiar *wham! wham! wham!* told her what it was.

"Terence," Mother said in a firm but quiet voice so that she would not awaken George. "Terence, you do not belong up here. You get right down and go to your bed in the carriage house."

Terence did not get down right away, but he looked at Mother with large, pleading eyes. "George was very lonely and sad tonight, Mother," Terence's large, pleading eyes said. His tail went *wham! wham! wham!*

Mrs. Ridgeway paused. She gave a reluctant sigh. Then she shut her eyes tight and tiptoed out of the room, closing the door behind her. "I didn't see a thing," she said to herself, "this one night."

XV. *Mice and Flowers*

On the morning of the mid-term examination in chemistry even Dorothy seemed to be nervous and excited. They had never seen Dorothy worried before, and it was troubling to observe that she could forget to put salt in the oatmeal and could leave the coffee percolating for fifteen minutes instead of the usual eight and a half.

"Are you scared you'll fail too, Dorothy?" asked Susan.

"Me?" said Dorothy, putting the dish towel neatly into the breadbox and the loaf of bread behind the stove. "No, I'm not scared, not at all. But that crazy big bozo, what's *he* going to do? Is he going to forget everything I tried to pound into him, or what?"

"I think he will remember," Susan said.

"I don't know," Dorothy said. "Sometimes I wonder, and in an examination I can't help him, I can't tell him. I can't even lift an eyebrow or wiggle a toe to help him to remember."

Dumpling came in from outdoors. Her eyes looked round and blue behind her shiny glasses. "Susy, do you know what?" she said.

"No, what?" said Susan absently.

"The birdseed is gone out of the cup in the birdcage, Susy!"

"Was Dickie there?"

"No-o," said Dumpling. "But, Susy, the birdseed **was** gone."

"Was the cage still on the ground?"

"Yes."

"Then it was mice," Susan said, "and don't tell George,

Dumpling, because it will just remind him and make him feel bad all over again."

"All right, Susy," Dumpling said.

Susan went upstairs to make her bed and get her books for school but Dumpling stood still and thought. "I was not good to canaries," Dumpling said to herself, "but I can be very, very good to mice." She went to the cupboard and got the birdseed package. She took it out behind the carriage house and carefully filled the birdseed cup and put the cup back in the open cage. She filled the water cup too. That would not stay quite full because the cage was lying on its side, but it could be partly filled without spilling, and Dumpling thought that the mice might like water as well as seed. After she had done this Dumpling looked up into the yellow tree. The breeze was swaying the yellow leaves, and one could almost imagine a yellow bird darting and fluttering there.

"Oh, Dickie, come back," Dumpling said. "I'm sorry I let you go." But only the leaves rustled, and there was not the twitter of a bird to be heard anywhere.

"Dumpling!" Susan called. "Time to get started for school, honey."

That afternoon, after the chemistry examination was over, Tommy walked home with Dorothy. The three Ridgeway children were watching for them, and they ran out to meet them. Everybody felt the terrible uncertainty and suspense.

"When will you know if you passed?" asked Susan.

"Not until Friday morning," Dorothy said. "It seems a long time."

"How do you *think* you did, Tommy?" asked George.

"It didn't seem hard," Tommy said, "but then exams never do seem hard to me. It's only afterwards that I find out."

"But he wrote a lot, didn't you, Tommy?" Dorothy said. "I know he can do it. I'm sure it was all right."

"Do *you* really think so?" Tommy asked.

"Yes, I do!" Dorothy said. She said it in that business-like way she had of speaking, and they all felt happier to have Dorothy say so. "Dorothy, I like you," Susan said. She had never been sure before. Dumpling came up beside Dorothy and took hold of her hand.

Later that afternoon the Ridgeway children saw Professor Jones of the Chemistry Department coming home with a bulging brief case. "He's got it!" George said. "He's got the examination papers. Susan, let's go over and find out."

"He doesn't care much for us, or football either," Susan said, "but I suppose we can try."

Mrs. Jones let them in with a look of doubt on her face. "He's got papers to correct," she said. "I don't think I'd go in there if I were you. Examination papers make him very cross."

"But that's why we came," Susan said. "It's about the papers."

They stood before Professor Jones in his study, and Susan said, "Please, sir, Mister-Professor-Doctor Jones—" She thought that if she used all his titles it might help to make him less cross.

"Someone has been picking my late chrysanthemums," said Mr. Jones accusingly. He was enthroned behind an amazing pile of examination books and he frowned sternly. "They are just beginning to bloom and they shouldn't be cut until frost, and someone has picked off two of the most promising—"

"We don't know who it was," said George. "It wasn't us."

"We're very sorry about your late chrysanthemums, Doctor Jones," Susan said.

"Just let me catch the culprit," Professor Jones said, "or culprits, as the case may be!"

"What we wanted to find out, please—" Susan said, but Professor Jones went on, "And furthermore, I see that you have recently acquired a dog. Now a dog is tolerable in its place, I daresay, and I can bear to see it grinning at me across the back fence. But if ever the said dog trespasses upon my property there is going to be trouble. And I don't mean maybe!"

"Yes, Mister-Professor-Doctor Jones," said Susan as politely as she was able under the circumstances.

"What we wanted to know—" said George, but just then the telephone on Professor Jones' desk rang.

"Hello," Professor Jones roared. "Athletic Department? No, this is Jones of Chemistry. Oh, you mean you're calling *from* the Athletic Department? Why don't you say so then?

Tucker? Tucker? I have no student named Tucker. Tokarynski? Yes, I have a student with that barbarous name, but I won't be rushed. I can tell you right now he has probably failed. No, that is not definite. I said *probably*, and I won't be rushed." He banged the receiver down.

"Well, I guess that's that," said Susan still as politely as she could. "We didn't mean to rush you, Doctor Jones. But it was just to find out if Tokarynski passed."

"Who is this chap Tokarynski?" Professor Jones bellowed.

"Oh," Susan cried, "the greatest football player Midwest ever had, Doctor Jones." And George said, "He's a quarterback."

"Well, I can tell you he's no chemist," said Professor Jones.

"But now," cried Susan, as she and George retreated toward the door, "*now*, he's learned to study! He's learned to study since the last exam."

"Scram," said Dr. Jones. He said it just as Dorothy did, only he didn't add, "Am-scray!" The Ridgeways scrammed.

"What did you find out?" asked Dorothy and Dumpling who had stayed at home.

"We didn't find out anything," George said. And Susan added sadly, "Examinations make him cross."

"We'll have to wait until Friday," Dorothy said, "when the grades will be posted."

"How many days until Friday, Susy?" asked Dumpling.

"Count on your fingers," Susan said. "It's four."

"Four days is long," Dumpling said.

Just then the doorbell rang. Susan and George and Dumpling ran to the door, and there stood the Terrible Torrences with bunches of flowers in their hands.

"Hello," said George. "What have you got there?"

"They are chrysanthemum-mums," said Alvin. And Rudy said, "Mum-mum-mums."

"What are you doing with them?"

"We are selling them," Alvin said, and Rudy said, "Ask your mama will she buy some nice fresh flowers."

"Just picked," said Alvin. And Rudy said, "Fresh."

"How much?" asked Susan.

"Whatever you want to pay," Alvin said, and Rudy said, "A dollar or ten cents or whatever you have handy."

"Mother," Susan called, "would you like to buy a nice bunch of fresh flowers for ten cents?"

"Not today, dear," Mother called back.

"Why are you selling flowers?" asked George.

"To get money," Alvin said. And Rudy said, "We are selling flowers to get money to give to you so that you can feed Terence."

"My goodness!" cried the Ridgeways in surprise.

"We are very nice little boys today," said Alvin. And Rudy said, "Like you told in the story, Susy."

"Well, for goodness sake!" said Susan in even greater

surprise. "Just a minute, Alvin and Rudy," Susan ran back in the house to consult Mother. "Mother!" she said, "the Terrible Torrences are trying to do something noble and good for once. I think we ought to help them."

"What are they doing?" asked Mother in alarm.

"They are selling flowers to get money to give to us to buy food for Terence!"

"But how wonderful!" cried Mother. "This I must see!"

She went to the door and looked down into the gentle and pious faces of the Terrible Torrences.

"Why, how very nice!" Mother said. "Quick, run for my purse, Susan."

"But, Mother," said George reasonably, "if we buy flowers from Alvin and Rudy so that they can give money to us, it really doesn't help us to feed Terence."

"That is so," Mother said. "Susan, you'd better not get my purse after all, dear."

"But it's a good idea," George said to the Torrences, "only you'd better go on down the street and sell the flowers to the other neighbors, and then you can bring the money back to us."

"Okay," said Alvin. And Rudy said, "We are very nice little boys today!"

"Are you very, very good?" asked Dumpling enviously.

"I think so," Alvin said. And Rudy said, "Sure, you bet."

"Professor Jones next door is very fond of chrysanthemums," Mother said. "Perhaps Mrs. Jones would like to buy some."

The Torrences looked doubtful. "Perhaps not," Alvin said. And Rudy said, "But we can try."

It was only after the Terrible Torrences had gone on down the street that Mother suddenly said, "Weren't some of Professor Jones' chrysanthemums exactly that shade of yellow?" And at the same moment George and Susan cried, "And somebody had been picking them!"

Dumpling sighed. "The Terrible Torrences were trying to be very, very good," she said.

"We had better go and see what happens," Susan said. And George cried, "Boy! Oh boy!"

Mrs. Jones had gone upstairs to sew, and when the doorbell rang Professor Jones had to leave his examination papers and answer it himself. This made him feel even crosser than he had been a few moments ago.

Susan and George and Dumpling caught up with the Terrible Torrences just as Professor Jones opened the door.

"Well," he roared, "what do you want?"

"We are selling flowers," said Alvin. And Rudy said, "We will sell you a bunch for anything you want to give, a dollar or ten cents or fifty-five cents or anything you have handy."

"Hmm!" said Professor Jones, soothed for a moment by the beauty of the flowers that the little Torrence boys were holding out to him. "Those are very fine specimens. Where did you get hold of flowers like those?"

"Down that-a-way," said Alvin, pointing in the general direction of the Jones' back yard. And Rudy said, "There are lots more where we got those. We can get you more."

A red wave of anger and suspicion surged across Professor Jones' countenance. "Down *which*-a-way?" he thundered in a voice that was full of emotion.

"Down *that*-a-way," said Rudy and Alvin together, pointing toward Professor Jones' back yard.

Professor Jones gave a cry that was between rage and anguish. "My chrysanthemums!" he cried. "My beautiful chrysanthemums!"

Too late the Terrible Torrences decided that they should not have tried to sell Professor Jones his own chrysanthemums. They turned and started to run, but there were the interested Ridgeways standing behind them and blocking their retreat. Professor Jones caught Alvin by the back of his shirt with one hand and Rudy by the back of *his* shirt with the other hand.

"Scram!" he roared to the Ridgeways, who scattered hastily out of the professor's path, and then closed in again behind as he marched Alvin and Rudy down the street to their home.

"Ring the doorbell for me, Dumpling, if you please," Professor Jones said.

"Okay," said Dumpling.

While they were waiting for Mrs. Torrence to answer the bell, Susan said, "Please, Professor Jones, I think they were trying to do good. They were going to give the money they earned to us to feed our dog."

"Dogs!" snorted Professor Jones. "Haven't I told you that I detest dogs?"

Mrs. Torrence looked frightened when she saw so many people at her front door. "Oh dear!" she cried, "whatever have they done now?"

"Madam," said Professor Jones, "they have picked my late chrysanthemums!"

"Oh, that was bad of them!"

"The question is," said Professor Jones, "how are they going to repay me for my loss?"

"Oh, dear!" Mrs. Torrence said, "I'll pay you whatever you ask, Mr. Jones."

"Not *you*, Madam," said Professor Jones. "*You* did not pick my choice chrysanthemums. But these boys did. They're not babies! They are big enough to know better. What are they going to do about it?"

Alvin and Rudy looked at Professor Jones, and Susan could not decide whether they were about to burst into tears or to shout "Yah! Yah! Yah!" and pretend to scalp him. What they did surprised her even more. For Alvin said, "We can wash dishes for you, Mr. Jones." And Rudy said, "We can wipe them, too."

"It entails a frightful risk to Mrs. Jones' china," said

Professor Jones, "but nevertheless I accept your offer. You may begin tonight, and you may wash our dishes every night for an entire week. At the end of that time, if you have conducted yourselves like young gentlemen I shall consider that you have paid me for the loss of my flowers, and I shall absolve you from any further blame."

"But they have never done dishes at home," cried Mrs. Torrence. "They've never done a thing to help. They won't know how at all."

"Then Mrs. Jones shall teach them," said Professor Jones. "I'll expect them tonight at six forty-five." And having said this, Professor Jones turned about and stalked away to his own house.

The Terrible Torrences always did the unexpected thing, and now they seemed quite pleased with themselves.

"Susan, we've got a job," Alvin said. And Rudy said, "We've got a job to wash the Jones' dishes, just like you've got a job to baby sit with us."

"Yes," Susan said, "you've got a job and you had better do it well and carefully. But I'll tell you something; and that is that my baby-sitting days are all over."

"Why, Susan?" they asked.

"Because you are big enough to look after yourselves."

"No more stories?" they asked sadly.

"I'll tell you stories when you come over to my house," Susan said, "if you will stop being terrible and acting like spoiled babies."

"Oh!" said the Terrible Torrences thoughtfully.

After supper Dumpling went out to put more birdseed in the birdseed cup. The mice or something had taken quite a lot of the seed that she had put into it that morning.

"I don't see any mice," Dumpling said to herself. "It is a mystery, like Mother writes. If Angus McAngus was here, he would tell if it is mice or squirrels or what that eats the birdseed." She thought about it awhile, and then she said, "But Angus McAngus is not here." She looked up into the yellow tree and she added sadly, "Neither is Dickie."

Dumpling looked over at Professor Jones' house and she could see a light in the study window and also one in the kitchen. She went to the hedge and looked across into the kitchen window, and she could see Alvin and Rudy washing Mrs. Jones' dishes. They had large gingham aprons tied around their necks, and they were very busy. Dumpling felt sorry for them. "I was not good to Dickie," Dumpling said to herself, "but I will be very, very good to the Terrible Torrences."

She went to the back door and knocked. Sometimes no child entered the house of the Joneses for months at a time, and suddenly there had been so many of them today that Mrs. Jones was quite taken aback.

"Dear me!" she said. "You, too, Dumpling?"

"I have come to help the Torrence boys do the dishes," Dumpling said.

So Mrs. Jones got another dish towel, and Dumpling

helped Rudy wipe while Alvin washed. Rudy and Alvin were busy telling Mrs. Jones a story.

"So there was this bad old man with a long blue beard and he hung his wives up in a little room by their hair," said Alvin. And Rudy said, "And the forty thieves lived in a cave in the mountain and when they wanted the door to open they said, 'Open, Sessy-sessy-something—' "

Mrs. Jones seemed somewhat bewildered, and she looked anxious too, Dumpling thought, about her nice china. But the Terrible Torrences did not break a thing.

"Thieves are nice in stories," Alvin said, "but they're not good to have around the house." And Rudy said, "It is better to wash people's dishes than to pick people's flowers if people don't want their flowers picked."

"But we didn't know that people didn't want their flowers picked," Alvin said. And Rudy said, "We are big boys and we do not need a sitter any more."

When the dishes were done, Alvin and Rudy said, "Good night, Mrs. Jones. We'll be back tomorrow." They went out the back door very quietly, and then they let loose and went up the street whooping like wild Indians.

Dumpling lingered behind. She went shyly to the door of Professor Jones' study and stood with the round part of her middle extending a little way into the room. The lamplight shone roundly and clearly on her glasses.

"Good evening," Dumpling said.

Professor Jones looked up in surprise. But he had had a

good dinner, he was nearly halfway through with the examination papers, and he felt considerably better than when the children had seen him earlier in the afternoon.

"Dumpling," he said, "you wouldn't pick a man's late chrysanthemums, would you?"

"No, I wouldn't," Dumpling said.

"I s'pose you've come about that fellow—what's his name?"

"Tokarynski," Dumpling said.

"Can you spell it?"

"No," Dumpling said. "Can you?"

"No," said the professor, "but I read his paper."

"Did he pass?" asked Dumpling.

"He passed," Professor Jones said. "It's a miracle, one of the seven wonders of the world! He couldn't have cheated because I had the seats all spaced out so they couldn't see each other's papers. Yet the fellow passed! Don't say the age of miracles is over, Dumpling."

"I won't," Dumpling said.

"And about the dog, Dumpling," the professor continued. "I don't object too greatly to a dog next door, if he does not dig holes under the hedge or howl at night."

"I will tell him," Dumpling said.

"You may go now, Dumpling," said Professor Jones.

"Okay," said Dumpling.

She ran so fast that she was all out of breath when she came into the kitchen.

"He passed," Dumpling said.

They looked at her in surprise, and Susan said, "Who, honey?"

"Why, Tommy of course," said Dumpling.

They all crowded around her.

"How do you know?"

"What makes you think so?"

"Where did you find out?"

"I asked Mr. Jones," Dumpling said, "and he told me."

They all began to pick her up and kiss her and waltz her around, and Terence barked, and Father came out of his study to find out what had happened, and Mother cried, "Good! Good!" and Dorothy just beamed and couldn't say a word.

"Then Tommy can play in the Homecoming game!" cried George. And Susan shouted, "Three cheers and a rah!"

Ever since she had let Dickie out of his cage, Dumpling had felt that while everybody still loved her and treated her politely she had somehow lost the special niche that she usually occupied as family saint. But now she had brought them good news, and she saw that they were proud of her once more.

XVI

Whose Dog?

On October thirty-first the Ridgeway children hauled all of the wooden boxes they had collected during the year up the street to the practice field. Already the students had made a pile as high as a tower that would be set afire after dark. Susan, George, and Dumpling saw with pleasure how their very own boxes were flung up here and there on the great pile to add to the brilliance of the evening. Then they hurried home to clear the yard as Father had told them to do. When everything was neatly stowed, so that Halloween or football pranksters could not find anything to carry away, they looked around with satisfaction.

"Oh boy! What a lot of room we would have to park cars, *if* we could park cars," George said.

"Four and one-half cars," Dumpling said.

"There's only one way we could ever get Daddy to let us park cars," Susan said, "and that is if Dean Ambrose would *ask* Father to let us do it."

"Ha! Ha!" George said scornfully. "That will happen when there are icicles on the sun."

"But how could icicles ever be on the sun?" asked Dumpling.

"George means it never will happen," Susan explained sadly.

They went over and looked at the Gimmicks' yard, and it was in the usual hopeless confusion.

"Oh boy! Oh boy! What a lot of things Halloweeners could carry off here," George said.

"Aren't you going to put away your things?" Susan asked.

"We can't," Tad said. "We have too many. Pop says Tim and me have got to take turns standing guard, so nothing gets took off."

"And can't you even go to the bonfire?" asked the Ridgeways.

"Yah," said Tim, "but we can't both go at once. We've got to take turns."

"You want to play in Leaping Lizard?" Tad asked. "We could play a picnic."

"With chorc'late cake!" said Tim.

"We can't today, thank you," Susan said, "because now we are going home to decorate our Tower for Homecoming."

"How are the Lizard's brakes?" asked George.

"Well, Pop hasn't got around to fixing them yet," Tim said. "We still don't dast to touch them."

"How you going to decorate your Tower?" asked Tad.

"Come over and see," Susan said. "We think we have a good idea."

"And Tommy Tucker's going to play!" George said. "You know that? Tommy Tucker's going to be in the Homecoming game!"

When they had finished decorating the Tower it looked very fine. Out of each window hung a ghost, and there were red and yellow paper streamers and the red and yellow pennant. A large sign with red and yellow crayon lettering said,

MIDWEST MAKES GHOSTS OF HER ENEMIES

Whenever a little breeze came rustling by, the five ghosts stirred and moved "as natural as life," George said.

"But ghosts are not alive," Dumpling said. Usually they would all have stopped and looked at her. But since she had let out the canary, what Dumpling said did not impress the others as much as it had. The light sparkled and shone on her glasses just as it used to do, but nobody seemed to be impressed.

"Anyway the ghosts look swell," the Gimmick boys said. "I wisht we had a Tower."

All up and down the street houses were being decorated and trimmed for Homecoming. The children walked up and down admiring them. Some of the fraternity houses where the men students lived had very wonderful decorations. One group of students had painted a great canvas stadium which covered almost the entire front of the house, and in the center, like football players, were dummies borrowed from a store and dressed in football suits.

Another group of students had carried corn shocks in from the country and set them up all over their lawn. In the midst of this they had put a very large scarecrow with black cardboard crows sitting on its shoulders. A sign said:

YOU CANNOT SCARE MIDWEST

When the children had looked at all the houses George said, "Nobody but us has ghosts."

"Maybe ghosts are not a good idea," said the Gimmick boys.

"It's because nobody else thought of mixing up Halloween with Homecoming," Susan said. "But I still think that it's a good idea."

In the afternoon judges went around to look at all the houses to see which ones were best.

"What if they forget to look at ours?" George asked.

"They will look at all of the houses," Susan said, "but I think that they will give the prize to the house with the painted stadium or the one with the scarecrow. We must not expect anything. If we expect too much we will be disappointed."

"That is something that they say in Sunday School," Dumpling said. Everybody stopped and looked at her for a second, but then they went on doing what they were doing without asking her to repeat the text.

As darkness fell people began to crowd College Avenue to look at the decorated houses. The fraternity houses had loudspeakers that carried the sound of jazz or boogie-woogie records out onto the October air. Sometimes a voice from inside the house would comment over the loudspeaker on the people who were passing by in the street. "Hi, Pete! Where's Sally tonight? Wow! Wow! What a pretty girl in that green coat! Hi, folks! There's Tommy Tucker! First time I ever saw Tommy with a girl! Who's your friend, Tommy? or friends? Why, Tommy's got the whole darn family with him!"

Of course it was only Dorothy and the Ridgeway children and the Terrible Torrences that Tommy Tucker was taking to the bonfire and the football rally.

"Tommy! They're talking about us, Tommy!" the Ridgeway children cried.

"Sure they are! You bet!" said Tommy, laughing and throwing out his chest. "We're something to talk about." Tommy was happy because he had made a first down in chemistry and could play in the Homecoming game.

As the Ridgeways passed the Gimmicks' yard they could see Tad sitting wistfully on the front porch of his house, watching the crowd go by to the football rally.

"Where's Tim?" asked George.

"He's gone to the rally," Tad said. "I've got to watch

until he comes back. When he comes back, I can go."

"I hope he remembers to come back," George said.

"I sure do hope he does," Tad said gloomily.

The Ridgeway children had not intended that Terence should go to the football rally. In fact George had given him a nice ham-bone as an extra treat and had shut him up in the carriage house. But even more than a juicy ham-bone Terence loved people and crowds and a lot of excitement. He could hear the sound of passing feet and blaring loudspeakers. By standing on his hind legs he could see through the carriage-house window that the children he adored were going away with the crowd. First Terence howled and barked, and then he clawed and scratched at the door. The carriage-house door closed with an old-fashioned latch. As Terence was leaping about and scratching and clawing his nose happened to bump and lift the latch. The door opened very easily, and Terence rushed out and down the street after George and Susan and Dumpling. He did not catch up with them until they had reached the practice field and the pile of boxes that would soon be lighted for the bonfire. Tommy Tucker had gone up onto the speakers' platform where the cheerleaders and the football coach and the other football players and important people were gathered. Dorothy was holding tight to Dumpling's hand so that Dumpling would not be lost in the crowd, and with the other hand she was holding Alvin, and he was holding Rudy. Susan and George stood next in a good place where they could hear all the speeches and also get a clear view of the bonfire. They were so busy looking at everything that they did not notice Terence until he put his front paws on George's shoulders and kissed George on the nose.

In his joy at finding them Terence would probably have knocked George right off his feet except that the crowd was so thick in this place that George was held up by it and did not have room to fall down.

"Oh dear!" Susan cried. "Terrence shouldn't have come at all! That's how he got lost before—in the midst of a football crowd!"

"You will have to take him home," Dorothy said.

"*Now?*" George cried in dismay.

"Yes, I think you had better," Dorothy said. "There will just be time before they light the bonfire. I'll stay here and keep the little kids, and you two take Terence home and shut him in the basement, and then come back. We will be right here."

"Terence, you are torrible!" scolded George, but Terence jumped up and down so happily that they could not really be angry with him. So Susan and George, with Terence between them, began pushing through the crowd on their way back home.

Strange children from far distant neighborhoods had walked or come by streetcar from all over the city to see the college bonfire. Some of these children were friendly and polite, but some of them were rude and noisy and in the worst kind of Halloween mood. Just as George and Susan and Terence were leaving the practice field a band of the rude and noisy kind of boys met them.

"Hey!" cried one of the strange boys in a loud voice. "Look there, Butch. Those kids have got our dog!" The boy called Butch began to call, "Here, Moose, Moose, Moose!"

Terence pricked up his ears and looked around. When he saw the strange boys rushing at him, his eager tail went down like a flag at half-mast. He began to press close against George and to make a funny growling, whining sound deep in his throat.

"This is *our* dog!" cried George. "His name is Torrible Terence."

"Torrible Terence!" roared the strange boys. "Gosh, what a name! He's our dog and his name is Moose."

"I am afraid," said Susan politely but firmly, "that you have made a slight mistake."

"Ho! Ho! Ho!" jeered the strangers. "She's afraid we've made a slight mistake! A slight—ho! ho! mistake. Didja hear that, kids? A slight—ho! ho! mistake!"

"Give us our dog, kids," said Butch. "You can't get away with takin' our dog."

"But he came to us," cried George, "and we advertised in the paper, and no one ever claimed him."

"I don't care! He's ours," the first boy said. "We lost

him at the football game two or three or four weeks ago."

"They can't even remember how long ago it was they lost their dog," said George scornfully.

"Well, see, he knows us! You can tell he does. Come here, you Moose, you! Get a wiggle on!" Butch raised his arm in a menacing gesture toward the dog, and Terence drooped his tail still farther and leaned hard against George.

"I'll tell you what," said George, "if you can call him and he goes with you, then we'll believe he's yours and you can have him."

"Here, Moose! Moose! Moose!" the boys began to call. George started to run toward home. "Here, Terence! Terence! Terence!" George called. Terence ran after George, leaping and bounding with joy and relief. "You see!" cried George triumphantly.

But Susan was worried. "Where do you live?" she asked the boys.

"Fifteen fifteen and a half North River Street," shouted one boy, "and you better bring our dog back there tomorrow or we'll tell the cops on you."

Susan ran after George and Terence, repeating the address to herself as she ran.

"I think he really was theirs, George," she said. "How terrible! How simply, really awful!"

"I don't care!" George cried defiantly. "He likes us best, Susy. Did you see how scared he was of that kid? They weren't good to him, Susy! They were mean to Terence."

"I know," Susan said, "but if he really belongs to them— oh dear!"

They shut Terence in the basement, where there was no latch that could easily be undone, and they poured out the tale of their adventure with the strange boys to Mother.

Mother wrote down the address that Susan remembered. "Tomorrow we will see about it," she said, "but this evening I'll keep Terence safe indoors and I am sure that everything will work out for the best."

"Oh, gee!" George wailed. "We lost the turtles and the canary! And now if Terence has to go too, and to people who will be mean to him! It isn't right, Mother. It isn't right."

"George," Mother said, "you can be sure that we will not do a thing that is not right, if we can help it. Now go back and enjoy the bonfire, dear. This ought to be a gay and happy evening."

XVII

More about the Lizard

There was a red glow on the sky as Susan and George started back to the rally, and they knew that the bonfire had been lighted. Coming and going on the wind was the wonderful *oom-pah-pah* of the college band playing "Forever, Dear Midwest." On the Ridgeways' Tower the five ghosts danced and shivered in the fitful breeze.

As they passed the Gimmick house, they saw that Tad was still sitting there, looking very disconsolate.

"Didn't Tim come back yet, Tad?" Susan asked.

"No, he didn't," Tad said. "He's gone and forgot." They could hear the sound of tears in Tad's voice.

"Gee!" George said. "That's too bad! But everybody's around the bonfire now. Surely nobody's going to come and carry off anything until the bonfire's over."

"And Tim will be back to watch by that time, won't he?" Tad said, wiping his eyes.

"I should think he would," said Susan. "We'll try to find him, Tad, and tell him to come back and let you go."

"I'll come with you," Tad said. "No one will bother the

place while the bonfire burns, and we'll find Tim and tell him to come home."

So the three of them hurried along together, forgetting their worries and troubles as they came nearer to the roaring, sparkling bonfire.

They were just in time to hear Tommy Tucker making his speech.

"Sure I'm going to play in the game tomorrow, folks," Tommy said, with the big grin everybody loved, and there was a roar of applause from all the listeners. "And there's something I've learned these last few weeks," Tommy went on when he could make himself heard. "You've got to hit the line hard, you've got to play for all you are worth; and I don't mean only in football, I mean in every kind of work you have to do; I mean in life too!"

"He means in chemistry too," said George, while the crowd roared its approval. Because of so many people, Susan and George and Tad could not get near to Dorothy and the younger children, but they could see them standing right beside the platform where Tommy was speaking. Dorothy was looking up at Tommy, and her eyes were very bright.

"Dorothy is proud," Susan said. "I don't blame her."

"And so tomorrow," Tommy said, "our team is going to do its very best for Midwest, and, folks, I think we're going to win the game."

There was another surge of cheering and applause, **and**

then the band began to play. The cheerleaders shouted
through their megaphones. The fire crackled and roared.
Then the cheerleaders started marching toward the fire,
one behind the other with their hands on one another's shoulders. Other people joined in, one after another with hands
on the shoulders of the person in front, so that they made
a long wavering line like a very large serpent. Other lines
started up too, and they wove in and out around the bonfire, chanting and cheering.

Susan and George and Tad forgot that they were looking
for Tim. They forgot that they might have pushed through
the crowd until they reached Dorothy. They attached themselves to the end of one of the long line of marchers and
went joyously serpentining all around the field, chanting:

> "Tucker! Tucker!
> Who's a good guy?
> Tokar-yn-ski!
> Hi! Hi! Hi!"

It was long past their usual bedtime, and the bright fire
was only a mound of glowing coals with sparks twirling
upward in the breeze, when it suddenly occurred to Susan
that they had better go home.

"Come on, George," she said. "Come on, Tad. We'd
better go home."

Other people seemed to have thought of the same thing
about the time that Susan did, and now there was a surge
of people all going away from the bonfire and toward their

homes. The three children went along with them, and now for the first time they began to feel tired and sleepy. The boys yawned and dragged their feet. "I'm glad we don't live far," Tad said. And George mumbled sleepily, "Stadium in our laps!" But as they came away from the practice field and around to the north side of College Avenue near the corner of the stadium, the crowd in which they moved was suddenly brought to a standstill. Traffic in the street seemed to be in some kind of a snarl.

"Sompun's happened," Tad said sleepily.

"I expect there's been an accident," said George with hope. He had already stopped yawning.

"It's just a car stalled," Susan said. "We'd better go around the other way and get on home. Mother will worry."

But the boys were already going under arms and between legs to get at the heart of the matter, and of course Susan had to follow. In the center of the crowded street they saw Officer Cahill and an abandoned jalopy. Officer Cahill had an electric torch in his hand and he was going over the car for license plates or marks of identification. There were plenty of marks of identification but no license plates. The light of the torch shone on the downhill slope of familiar letters, Leaping Lizard.

"Lizard!" the children cried. And Tad, in stricken accents, wailed, "Oh, gosh!" Some prankster had pushed the Lizard out of the Gimmicks' yard and left it standing in the middle of the busy street.

"Who owns this car?" shouted Officer Cahill. Nobody seemed to know until the three children arrived. "You know who owns this car?"

"Sure," the children said. They all began to talk at once. "Someone must have stole it out of our yard—it's Mr. Gimmick's—don't ever touch the brakes—its name is Lizard—"

"We've got to get it out of here," Officer Cahill said. They were surrounded by the honking of impatient car horns and the shouts of pedestrians.

Tad said, "Golly! I was s'posed to watch it!"

"Got to push it to the curb until the crowd gets by," Officer Cahill said.

"We'll help you push," cried George and Tad. Other people helped too. The old car rolled along easily. Apparently no one had made the mistake of setting the brakes. George began to make "Beep-beep!" and "B-r-r-r-r! Ker-atch!" noises as he hove his shoulder to.

Susan was looking around. Exactly ahead of them was the break in the curbing through which Dean Ambrose's car always passed to reach the snug berth which it occupied between the corner of the street and the rounded wall of the stadium.

"Steady now," the officer said to the owners of the many helping hands. "Steady now. Ease her along into this hole. Take her slow."

"Mr. Cahill!" Susan cried, "that's the place where Dean Ambrose always parks his car on football days."

"That there's the Dean's small hole," cried Tad.

"So what?" said Officer Cahill. "We'll whisk it out bright and early tomorrow morn. Heave away, lads!"

The Leaping Lizard rolled gently and easily into the Dean's favorite parking place.

"She's rollin' backward," someone called. "You better set them brakes, Officer."

"Right-o!" said Officer Cahill cheerily.

"Don't touch the brakes," shouted George and Susan. And Tad yelped, "No! No! No! Keep yer hands off them brakes. I'm going to get the works anyway without you set the brakes."

As if he had not heard either of them, and perhaps he hadn't for everyone was shouting and offering advice, Officer Cahill reached into the jalopy and gave the handle of the emergency brake a mighty pull. There was a kind of grinding and falling sound, not loud but ominous.

"There," said Officer Cahill. "In the morn we'll swish it out of here, and tell your Daddy not to worry, Tad, my boy. She'll be as safe as a bank!" He went to the center of the intersection, blew his whistle, and began to sort and disentangle the bleating traffic.

The three children went across the street and down the block toward home.

"He'll never get it out of there in the morning at all, at all!" cried Tad. "Oh, glory! Will I get the works!"

"They'll have to get it out before the football game," George said, "because that's where the Dean always and forever parks his car. He never bothers to come early to find a parking place, because he knows they keep this little hole especially for him."

"I ain't worrying about no Dean," said Tad. "I'm worrying about me."

Susan said nothing at all, but her mind was very active.

"What's the matter, Susy?" George asked. "Are you worried too?"

"No, I was thinking," Susan said. "I was thinking, what would Dean Ambrose do if he should roll up late tomorrow to the game and find no place to park?"

"I guess he would go home again," George said.

"And not use his ticket? And miss the game?" asked Susan.

"He would be awful mad," George said.

"But *if*," said Susan, "he saw that there was one empty driveway left, one real good place to park—"

"The Ridgeways' turnabout!" yelped George.

"I sure do hope those brakes didn't lock!" Tad was saying mournfully to himself.

Susan and George looked at Tad and they were sorry for him. But Susan couldn't help repeating something she had once read in an old copybook, "It's an ill wind that blows nobody good."

XVIII

North River Street

It was a beautiful Saturday morning again and the day of the Homecoming game.

"But this morning," Mother said, "we have something besides football to think of. We must settle once and for all the question of who owns Terence."

"Oh dear!" Susan said.

"Mother, he was afraid of those boys," George cried. "He didn't want to belong to them."

"Nevertheless," Mother said, "it must be settled. As soon as your morning chores are done, Daddy will drive you and Terence down to this address on North River Street and find out what the situation really is."

"Oh, Susan," George said, "I wish you hadn't asked for the address."

"But we have to do what is right," Susan said sadly.

Terence loved to ride in the car and he leaped in eagerly without any urging. He almost filled the back seat, and George could barely squeeze in beside him. Susan and Dumpling sat on the front seat with Father. George put his arm around Terence's neck, and Terence kept turning around to give George enthusiastic kisses with his long wet tongue. His tail went *wham! wham! wham!*

"He doesn't know where he's going," George said. "He thinks it's all for fun."

It was a long way from College Avenue to North River Street, and, when he was not kissing George, Terence hung his head out of the window and sniffed all of the strange and different smells along the way. When they came near 1515½ North River Street the smells were quite different. There was the damp, weedy smell of the river, and the oily smell of a linseed oil factory, and the smoky smell of trains from the railroad bridge that crossed overhead. Terence sniffed again and his tail stopped whamming. He began to tremble and to lean hard against George.

"Oh, Daddy!" George cried. "Please drive on by. He doesn't want to stop."

"George," Father said, "some things are hard to do. But just because a thing is hard we must not turn away from it, if it is right."

"Chemistry was hard," Dumpling said, "but Tommy didn't turn away from it, did he, Daddy?"

Boys were playing ball in the street in front of 1515½ North River Street. They came around the Ridgeways' car and looked in as the car stopped.

"Geez! It's the Moose!" they said in wonder. "It's our dog. They brung him back!"

"Pop'll give you heck, kid," one of the boys said. "He don't never want to see—"

"Is your father at home, boys?" Professor Ridgeway asked. "I'd like to speak to him if he isn't busy."

"Busy?" said one of the boys, laughing. "No, he ain't never busy!"

"Pop!" they yelled. "Get your britches on and come down."

The house was a very old one, as old as the house the Ridgeways lived in, but it had not had the loving care that had been given to the old house on College Avenue. There was no grass in the beaten dooryard, the shingles were falling off the roof. The house had not been painted for so long that one could no longer imagine what the color had been. The ½ was the upstairs part of the house, and presently down the rickety outside stairway came a redfaced man in a dirty undershirt and stained overalls.

"What's the matter?" he asked crossly.

"Pop, they've brung back Moose. Can we have him, Pop?"

The man came up beside the car. "That ain't our dog," he said.

"He is too, Pop!" cried the boys. "You know he is!"

"Well, then we don't want him," said the man. "He eats more'n we do. We can't afford to feed him."

"We can't afford to feed him either," Father said. The Ridgeway children drew long sighing breaths, and George's sigh was more like a sob. Father went on, "But, although we really can't afford to feed him, we *do* want him. Which one of you boys is the owner of this dog?"

"I am," said the boy called Butch. "But Pop won't let me have him up to bed with me. He kicks him down them stairs whenever he comes up."

"What's your name?" Father asked.

"It's Butch," the boy said.

"Well, Butch," said Father, "we want to buy this dog from you."

"Buying, is it?" said the man in surprise. "Well, now he's *my* dog too. He belongs to the whole family of us, and mighty fond of him we was, when we had the stuff to feed him."

Professor Ridgeway put his hand in his pocket and drew out a bill. He pushed aside the man's reaching hand and held the money out to Butch.

"Butch," he said, "will five dollars recompense you for the loss of your dog?"

"Golly, yes!" said Butch. "I can buy me a good warm jacket for school with that there money. I guess he's happier with you anyway. Hey, Moose?"

He put his hand in the window and touched the dog's head.

"His name is Torrible Terence," Dumpling said.

"Hey, Terence, fellow?" Butch said wistfully. Terence licked Butch's hand and then he turned and rubbed his head against George.

"Is it all right then, Butch?" George asked.

"Ya, you bet," Butch said. And so the Ridgeways drove back again to College Avenue, and all the way back Terence's tail went *wham! wham! wham!* with joy.

"Thank you, Daddy," George said. "Five dollars is a lot of money. It would buy a lot of dog food."

"But Butch will have a warm jacket," Susan said, "and now we really own Terence. We won't have to worry any more. He is our own dog."

"We will just have to worry how to feed him," Dumpling said.

"If we could only earn money parking cars—" Susan began, but after Father had been so good as to buy Terence for them, she was immediately sorry that she had raised the old question of parking cars. But Father was not angry.

"I am not personally opposed to your parking cars on football days, Susan," Father said gravely. "It is just that I am sure Dean Ambrose would not approve. We'll feed Terence and get along somehow, even if we have to do without a few of those delicious doughnuts and cookies Mother makes for us. We're not badly off, you know. A trip to North River Street once in a while is very good for us, I think. It makes us realize how really fortunate and happy and well off we are."

XIX

Concerning Dean Ambrose

While the Ridgeways were at lunch the doorbell rang, and one of Tommy Tucker's friends stood there with an envelope in his hand and a box from the florist shop.

"Here are three tickets to the football game," he said, "and a corsage for Miss Sturm."

"For me?" said Dorothy. "For pity's sake!"

"But I thought that every seat in the stadium was sold out for today," Father said.

"Well, Tommy could only get three tickets, and he said to tell you that he was sorry, because he wanted to get six so that all of you could go. He said that you could divide the three tickets up any way you cared to, only he thought that Dorothy—that is, Miss Sturm—had really earned one of them."

"Dorothy, will you go?" the children cried. "You won't have to study, will you, Dorothy? You'll go and wear the corsage?"

"No, I'm not going to study today," Dorothy said. "I'm getting kind of interested in football."

"Three tickets to the game!" cried Mother. "That's really splendid! Dorothy must go, of course, and then I think that George and Susan might go too, don't you, Daddy?"

"Yes," Father said, "I think they should, and Dumpling won't mind watching from the Tower with us, will you, Dumpling?"

"No," Dumpling said. "Irene and I would rather play house anyway."

George and Susan had begun to jump and shout with joy, but then they looked at each other, and several important thoughts chased themselves rapidly through their minds. "What if Dean Ambrose comes looking for a parking place!" George thought. And Susan thought, "Mother and Daddy have lived here right beside the stadium for so many years, and I don't believe they've ever gone to a game since they had us to look after. I'll bet they'd like to go."

"Oh, Mother!" Susan said, "George and I like watching games from the Tower, don't we, George?"

"Sure," George said. "We would stay, and you could go."

"Oh, no," Mother said.

"Oh, Mother, yes!" cried Susan.

"What do you think, Daddy?" Mother asked a little wistfully.

"Well," Father said, "if they don't really care—it would be quite a lark!"

"Oh, and Daddy," Susan said, "you must get Mother a corsage, and that would make it really wonderful."

"A corsage!" Mother said, her cheeks looking pink and her eyes excited. "My goodness, no! What an extravagance!"

"Susan," Daddy said, "you have extremely good ideas. But really, wouldn't you and George be disappointed?"

"No, Daddy! No!" they cried. George and Susan looked at each other and smiled. Although they would have enjoyed sitting in regular seats in the big stadium, they were satisfied that it had turned out this way.

"Oh, what fun!" Mother said. "Oh, Dorothy, aren't you excited? We're going to the game and wear corsages. Oh, my!"

"We'd better am-scray then," Dorothy said, pretending to be calm about everything. "We've got these lunch dishes to do, and lots of things before we're ready to go."

"Oh, goodness yes!" Mother said. "What a lark! Oh, hurry, hurry, hurry!"

"Don't rush, dear," Professor Ridgeway said. "At least, living this near the stadium, we can take our time. We won't have to park a car. We can leave home after the crowds have gone by and arrive just in time for the kick-off."

"As late as Pinkie Ambrose," Mother said happily. And Father was too excited to remind her that Pinkie Ambrose was a Dean.

The Ridgeway children made themselves unusually neat and tidy for a Saturday afternoon. Susan combed her own hair and tied fresh red ribbons on Dumpling's pigtails.

"Why, Susy dear," asked Dumpling, "if we are only going to the Tower?"

"We must be neat and refined," said Susan.

"Why, Susy?" persisted Dumpling.

"We hope to see the Dean," Susan said.

George had made several scouting expeditions to the corner of the stadium, returning to report to Susan that the Lizard was still there. "Boy! Is it ever there!" he said, adding with relish, "and boy! oh boy! are Mr. Gimmick and Officer Cahill mad! They've been trying all morning to move the Lizard out of there."

"Poor Tad!" Susan said. But George said, "Susy, it wasn't Tad that got the works. It was Tim because he forgot to come back."

At one-fifteen the stream of football fans passing the Ridgeway house began to grow thinner. Belated cars were still cruising the streets to find a parking place, but in general things were quieting down. The Gimmicks' driveway was full of cars, and Tad and Tim had taken in their signs. Mother was still hurrying into her things, and Dorothy was getting her corsage out of the box; and Father had just come back with another corsage for Mother. The three Ridgeway children sat in an expectant row on the stone wall in front of the house.

Occasionally a worried motorist would slow his car and shout at them, "Hey! Can I park in your drive?"

"I'm very sorry," Susan replied politely, "but our father does not allow us to park cars."

"There he is!" George said. "There's the Dean!"

"Don't point," said Susan. "It isn't dignified."

Dean Ambrose raised a hand in absent-minded greeting as he rolled leisurely by. He was flushed with a good lunch taken at his ease, and he expected to drive right into his parking place and go into the stadium and have a pleasant afternoon.

The children watched him roll by, and waited.

"Of course," said George uneasily, "he might find some-place else."

"He might," said Susan.

Father came out on the porch. "Why aren't you fans in the Tower?"

"The game hasn't started yet," said Susan. Father went back into the house. "Mother," he called, "for pity's sake, hurry! No one will notice if your lipstick's on crooked."

The Dean's car came down the street again. It was going faster now, and the Dean's face was several shades redder. It had lost its expression of calm repose.

"Just a minute, darling," Mother called. "I can't find my winter gloves. I'm sure there's lots of time."

The Dean looked at the Ridgeway children as he drove by. This time he did not raise a hand in greeting but he noticed their empty driveway with a look of great interest. Still he went on by.

"Maybe we should have had a sign," George said.

"No, we must be patient," Susan said. "He has to come to us. We mustn't go to him."

"I s'pose you're right," George said. But it was very hard to wait.

The third time the Dean came around the block he was certainly exceeding the speed limit. His face was fiery red and his mouth was working. With a shrieking of brakes he pulled up in front of the Ridgeway house and shouted in a loud voice to the Ridgeway children, "How about parking in your driveway?" George gave an enthusiastic yelp which was just about to turn into a "Sure!" when Susan pushed him firmly aside.

"I'm very sorry, Dean Ambrose," Susan said in a sweet, clear voice, "but our father does not allow us to park cars."

"He doesn't allow—?" roared the Dean. "Why not?"

Susan could hear Father and Mother coming out on the porch behind her. It was all happening very nicely, just like a play.

"Because," Susan said in her most polite but clear voice, "because our father feels that it is not very dignified for faculty children to park cars. He feels that a great University like Midwest expects something better of professors' children."

"Ridgeway!" roared the Dean. "Do you mean to say that you are deliberately holding out parking space on football days in this congested area, because—because of—"

"Because of adachemic dignity," said Dumpling.

"Ridgeway, where is your Midwest spirit?" wailed the Dean. Father and Mother and Dorothy had come out now and were standing beside the children on the sidewalk. Father cleared his throat and spoke.

"Children," said Father, "will you kindly park the Dean's car in our driveway and charge him the customary twenty-five cents?"

"Are you sure, Father?" asked Susan.

"Yes, I am sure," said Father.

George was already making "Stop," "Go," and "Come ahead a few inches" motions in the best style of Officer Cahill. The Dean's car rolled into the driveway and up to the turnabout.

"Well!" said the Dean, as if it was about time.

Three or four other cars had slowed up hopefully behind the Dean's car and were tooting to be let in.

"One at a time, please," Susan said. "We can take only three more of you, and it will be a quarter for each car, if you please."

"Well, Pinkie," Mother said, as she and Father and the Dean and Dorothy started off toward the stadium. "It's a long time since we've seen a game together."

"A-hem!" said the Dean, clearing his throat for a serious remark, but what it was the Ridgeway children never knew because for a few moments they were far too busy parking cars. They could scarcely believe it, but presently there were four cars lined up neatly in their driveway! And Father and the Dean had really insisted on it!

"And look at here!" George cried. "Four quarters. That's a dollar, and it will buy quite a lot of dog food."

"Next week too?" asked Dumpling.

"I think so," Susan said. "I don't think anyone will ever make a fuss again about our parking cars."

"How many more football games?" asked Dumpling.

"Two," Susan said, "but there will be football again next fall."

"Three dollars," George said, "that will not be enough money to feed Terence until next fall."

"Well, it will help," Susan said. "It's better than nothing. And we have the fun of parking cars, just like the Gimmicks."

"Boy!" George said. "Did you see me directing traffic, telling them how to park? Just like Officer Cahill."

"Yes, I saw," Susan said. "And now we'd better hurry to the Tower. They've begun to let the balloons fly away. The game must have started."

XX. A Number of Things

Watching with the field glasses from the Tower, it seemed to the Ridgeway children that there had never been a better football game. Certainly Tommy Tucker had never played a finer game. He always seemed to be in that part of the field where he was needed most. Now he had intercepted the ball and carried it for a first down. Now he had carried it over the goal line and made a touchdown.

"Dorothy will be proud," Susan said. And George said, "We're proud too!"

At the end of the first half of the game, Midwest was far ahead of the visiting team, and the cheering from the stadium came to the children like a roar of thunder. Red and yellow balloons from the kickoff still floated lazily in the blue October sky. A particularly nice red one came nearer and nearer to the Rideways' Tower. Presently a little puff of air brought it so near that George could stretch out his hand and grasp the string and pull it in the window above the gently stirring ghosts. "Oh boy! Oh boy! Oh boy!" cried George, and he was very happy.

In the period between the halves of the football game, while the members of the two teams were resting, the Midwest band marched onto the football field to play the college songs. One of the college girls had been chosen Homecoming Queen for that day, and as the band played "Forever Dear Midwest" the queen came onto the field in her crown and robes and was introduced to everyone in the stadium. The children could see her plainly through the field glasses, and how very pretty she was. They could see the president of the student body who was introducing her, and over the radio they could hear what he said.

When he had finished introducing the queen, he said, "And now, ladies and gentlemen, there is just one more announcement I wish to make before the game goes on. Many people all up and down College Avenue have decorated their houses in honor of Homecoming, and at this time we wish to tell you which houses received the awards of the judges."

George and Susan and Dumpling came and stood close beside the radio, so that they would not miss a word.

"The first prize of twenty-five dollars," said the speaker, "goes to the Delta Phi Omega house for its fine display."

"That's the one with the stadium," Susan said.

"Oh, gee!" George said.

"But it's right that they should have it, George," Susan said. "That one was the best."

"The second prize of fifteen dollars," said the speaker, "has been awarded to the Alpha Eta Pi house with its cornfield and its scarecrow."

"Oh, gee!" George said.

"But, yes," Susan said sadly, "I guess they really did deserve it, George."

"Both of these prizes," said the speaker, "have been awarded to large houses where groups of students live together. In awarding the third prize, the judges decided that the ten dollars should go to a private house instead of a fraternity house."

"Oh boy, oh boy!" said George.

"Many private houses," continued the speaker, "were beautifully and tastefully decorated, and we wish to thank the owners for their interest and cooperation. But the private house with the most original and interesting decorations, in the opinion of the judges, was the one which combined the idea of Halloween with the idea of Homecoming. Folks, the third prize of ten dollars goes to the house at Seventeen-forty College Avenue, the house with the tower and the five ghosts."

There was a great roaring cheer from the stadium, and whether it was because the Ridgeway children had won the ten dollars or because the football team had chosen that moment to return to the field for the second half of the game, no one could say. But George and Susan and Dumpling cheered too, and long after the game had been resumed, they were still cheering and leaping about and hugging Terence and each other, and crying, "Boy! Oh boy! What a wonderful day!"

It was a wonderful day in more ways than one, for it turned out to be the greatest football victory that Midwest had ever known, and all because of Tommy Tucker's splendid playing.

The Gimmick boys and the Terrible Torrences joined the Ridgeway children on the Ridgeway lawn to watch the crowd leaving the stadium and to talk over all the exciting things that had happened.

They all sat on the stone wall, and it is true that Tim sat

down very carefully, for it turned out that "the works" had been applied rather violently to the part of Tim that went down first when he sat. Mr. Gimmick believed in the old saying, "Spare the rod and spoil the child," and he did not intend to see Tim spoiled.

"What about the Leaping Lizard?" Susan asked.

"Pop says he'll have it out of there tonight after the crowd's gone," Tim said. "And you know what? He says it's no good as a car anyway, and he's going to put it far back out of the way in our yard, and lock the brakes and let it stay there, and all of us can use it just to play in."

"Us too?" asked George.

"Sure," said Tad, "even the Torrences. We can pretend all kinds of trips and picnics too!"

"With chorc'late cake," said Dumpling.

Just then Father and Mother and the Dean and Dorothy came back from the game. They looked as if they had been having a good time.

"Ridgeway," the Dean said, "you have the nicest little family I ever saw. Well-behaved children! Yes, well-behaved children. I hope you will let them park my car for me every week. This is a much better spot than that small corner by the stadium."

Father smiled. "I'm sure they'll be glad to take care of your car for you, Dean Ambrose, at any time. They are very, very good children."

"But it's hard always to be very, very good," Dumpling

said, remembering how she had tried to be very, very good to Dickie. "It is hard to have to be a P-R-O-D—one of those things."

"Oh, darling," Mother said, "that reminds me that I sat next to one of the young ladies from the Child Study Clinic at the football game, and she said, 'How is that nice little girl of yours who is so good at puzzles?' and I said, 'Dumpling is fine, but do tell me! She isn't a prodigy, is she? Because I think I shouldn't like to have her be anything so unusual.' 'Oh, no,' the young lady said. 'We did have a sort of child prodigy in for testing that same morning that Dumpling was in. Dumpling is certainly above the average in smartness, but she is not a prodigy.' "

Dumpling caught hold of Mother around the waist. Her eyes sparkled behind her glasses. Her pigtails bristled with pleasure and relief. "Mummy," she said, "you mean that I don't *always* have to be very, *very* good?"

"Why, honey-child," Mother said, "not very, *very* good— just good the way you've always been. Just be our usual Dumpling."

A great weight seemed to have lifted off Dumpling's mind. She skipped and hopped and ran all around the front yard. She went in the house and got Irene and said to her, "Irene, honey, we're not that P-R-O-D thing they said at all. And if we just be good it's enough without the very, *very*."

While the others were still talking and laughing and being happy in the front yard, Dumpling and Irene went out behind the carriage house and looked at Dickie's cage. The seed was gone out of the cup. "Those mice," Dumpling said, "they must be awfully hungry."

She threw back her head and looked up into the tree. Almost all of the yellow leaves had fallen since yesterday. Any day now the winter cold would be beginning. There were still a few yellow leaves left, and suddenly one seemed to detach itself and float on the air. But it did not float gently down as other falling leaves did. It went to another branch and attached itself there. "Tweet! tweet! tweet!" it said quite musically. Dumpling looked and then she rubbed her eyes and looked again. She drew a deep breath and stood very still. The yellow leaf which had spoken "tweet" detached itself again from the branch and came down, down, down, right to the entrance of the open bird cage. It paused a moment, and Dumpling held her breath. Then it went hop, hop, hop into Dickie's cage, pecked at the birdseed cup, tried the water cup, and then it hopped very lightly onto the swing which went sideways in quite a funny way because, after all, the cage was lying on its side.

Dumpling's heart began to pound with excitement. She moved very softly toward the open cage. When she was quite near to it, she suddenly turned it right side up, so that the top of the cage sat on the bottom part, just as it should do. And there inside the cage was Dickie! He began to scold her and flutter his wings and jump about just as he used to do. But Dumpling was no longer fooled by Dickie's actions.

They were all surprised to see Dumpling coming around the house with the birdcage clasped firmly against that part of her which stuck out farthest.

"Susy," she cried, "you were wrong about mice."

"Wrong about mice?" asked Susan, puzzled. But Dumpling went on to George, and she said, "George, I gave you turtles for a birthday present and you had to let them go—"

"Dickie!" cried George. "Why, Dumpling, where did you find him?"

"He came back," Dumpling said. "This is his home. And don't worry, George. If he flutters and makes a fuss he doesn't really want to get out, it's just the way he acts."

"Boy, oh boy!" said George.

"And now he belongs to you, George," Dumpling said, "to make up for the turtles. Happy birthday, George."

The Terrible Torrences began to sing:

> "Happy birthday to you!
> Happy birthday to you!
> Happy birthday, dear Georgie,
> Happy birthday to you!"

Rudy said, "Will there be a cake?" And Alvin said, "With candles?"

"Yes," Mother cried, "there will just be time before dinner to bake a cake. Don't you think so, Dorothy?"

"Yes," Dorothy said, "I'll run right in and start the oven."

"And you are all invited to dinner," Mother said. "Tim and Tad and Rudy and Alvin, run ask your mothers if you can stay, because we have a great many things to celebrate today, and Tommy Tucker is coming to supper with us too!"

"Hooray!" everybody shouted.

"But *we* will have to leave early," Alvin said. And Rudy said proudly, "Because *we* have to do the Jones' dishes."

"Certainly," Mother said.

"And you can have candles if you want to," Alvin said. And Rudy said, "Because we are big boys now, aren't we, Susan? And we would not act like Eskimos and eat the candles, would we?"

"No," Susan said, "because you are big boys."

So everybody began to bustle around and help prepare for dinner. Dickie's cage was hung back on its hook, and George turned somersaults all around the living room, and Terence ran after him, barking and trying to kiss his nose.

"We live in a madhouse," Mother said, as she whipped up the eggs for the cake, "but it is a very nice one!"

"Mother," Susan said, "are you still stuck in the middle of your mystery story?"

"Yes," Mother said, "but I suppose it doesn't really matter, because everything else seems to be turning out so well today."

"I've been thinking," Susan said, "why don't you have the Countess the one who really stole the diamond necklace?"

Mother stopped whisking eggs and looked at Susan in surprise. "But, Susan," she said, "the diamond necklace belongs to the Countess!"

"I know," Susan said, "and that is why it would be such a surprise to everybody and why nobody would guess."

"Dear me!" said Mother, "but why?"

"Maybe she wanted to collect insurance on it, or maybe she just wanted some excitement or something. Surely you could think of reasons."

"Yes, I could!" Mother said. "Please, Dorothy, finish whisking the eggs. I'll be with you again in a minute." She began jotting notes on the scratch pad where she usually wrote her grocery lists. "Countess stole own necklace," she muttered as she scribbled, "to keep it from falling into the hands of wicked brother-in-law who was real murderer of Countess's husband. Angus McAngus finds clue—"

"The eggs are whisked, Mrs. Ridgeway," Dorothy said.

"Fine! Fine!" Mother cried, returning to the cake dough, and beginning to fold in the whites of eggs. "Susan, whatever made you suspect the Countess?"

"I think it was Dickie," Susan said. "The birdseed was being stolen and we suspected the mice, but all the time it was Dickie, himself."

"Susan," Mother said, "I will teach you how to use the typewriter. *You* shall write the novels for the family."

"No," Susan said, "I'd rather tell and let you write. But maybe we can work together."

Just then there was a great shout from the back door. Tommy Tucker had arrived, fresh from a shower bath in the athletic dressing room. He had a crisscross bit of adhesive tape on his left cheek and a red spot of Mercurochrome over his right eye, and he was smiling his wide, nice smile. Behind him rushed the Gimmicks and the Torrences, and George and Terence and Dumpling and Susan rushed at him from inside the house.

"Tommy! Tommy! Tommy!" they shouted.

"Hey!" cried Tommy. "What kind of scrimmage is this? I've had enough tackling for one day."

"Tommy, we won't tackle! We'll be your guard," they cried. "Come in! Come in! We'll all be very good to you."

"Dorothy too?" asked Tommy.

Dorothy was peeling potatoes at the kitchen sink, but she turned around and smiled at all of them, and she seemed to have forgotten how to say "Am-scray!"

And so it was a lovely party.

DATE DUE

DEC 11	OCT 17	MAY 25	T
DEC 15	OCT 24	SEP 16	
	NOV 28	SEP 24	
JAN 9	APR 8	OCT 9	
JAN 20	MAY 16	APR 25	
MAR 18	SEP 12	DEC 1	
MAY 13		DEC 8	
MAY 20	SEP 26	JAN 21	
NOV 11	OCT 18		
	NOV 13	OCT 15	
JAN 24	FEB 7	JA 9 '86	
MAR 28			
MAY 18	MAR 30	APR 8 '86	
SEP 27	MAY 15	FEB 29 '88	

Bri   22441

Brink
Family grandstand